I NEVER STOPPED

ELIZABETH MITCHELL

I NEVER STOPPED

Published in the United States by Little Key Press.

ISBN: 978-1-949990-52-2
First Edition

Edited by Tessa Garrett
Cover Designed by Elizabeth Mitchell with images from:
Lesley found on Pexels
Matthew Henry found on Unsplash

To the man I'll never stop loving,
Wesley

1

SLOANE

After

Francesca crumpled at the sound of Sloane's name, the smell of her sweaters, the honk of their model-car home phone, even leftovers she refused to deal with in their refrigerator.

Sloane watched and trudged through a surrounding muck as though a failing iron lung breathed for her. With a hazy filter tinting Sloane's world, an emptiness settled in next to the pain.

Being silenced by fog, Sloane could deal with, but the desperation to see a slight impression where she lay or see a wisp of Francesca's hair move when she attempted to brush it from her face consumed her. Sloane tried to rub her back or wrap herself around Francesca as she always did–forever the big spoon–but she'd slip right through.

The first time it'd happened, the first time her hand had slid through Francesca's, Sloane's scream could have ripped the universe open. She'd exploded, the sensation akin to dropping from the top of a roller coaster. Each time following made her gasp; each time her sounds were swallowed.

For months, all Sloane could do was break into pieces–with Francesca, but without her; beside her, but missing her skin's warmth.

FRANCESCA SAT in her large leather chair, wrapped in a cable-knit blanket. A book lay on the stacked wine box table beside her, open and faced down.

Sloane gently cupped Francesca's cheek. "It'll be alright, my love. I'll figure something out, I promise. I've been working on it."

With a start, Francesca cracked swollen brown eyes open and let shaky fingers brush her face as she looked around. "Sloane?" Wiping her freckled face dry, she admonished herself aloud. "Sure. Haven't you only wished that a thousand times?" Francesca hated waking up–she'd cried that out so many times it rattled in Sloane's head like loose dice. Francesca's voice became small. "Sloane? I miss you. I've said that so many times by now you'd have told me to shut up." A barely noticeable smile flashed.

Sloane nodded shakily. "I wish we could be saying our, 'I love you's,' not 'I miss you's,'" she said–but her words were sucked up. Only she could hear herself now.

Could Francesca remember the sound of her voice? She wouldn't watch videos of them like they used to do.

Did she even remember Sloane's face? Francesca hadn't been able to glance at pictures after she'd ripped collages from walls, knocked frames from shelves, and tore magnetic vacation snapshots from the freezer door with an overwhelming heartache that cracked through and shook the nearly-there place that held Sloane–the place she called The Gray.

Sloane had shivered with Francesca's pain.

Francesca tried once, just to peek at a Polaroid being used as a bookmark in a collection of poetry they'd read to each other. As blood-curdling as the night of the crash, she cried Sloane's name out like a prayer, a curse, a plea. Sloane's attempts to calm Francesca were frustratingly lost in The Gray.

Sloane remembered trying to respond the night of the accident too. She would have sworn she'd called out, "I'm here, my love. What's happened? I'm here. I'm here."

Instead of answering, Francesca had ripped the grass, clawed at it with bleeding hands and screamed for Sloane who kneeled beside her.

They'd seen Sloane's body at the same time.

2

BEFORE

Francesca

Branches cracked and shifted the air in jagged patterns. Heaving breaths and an unsteady heartbeat echoed loud, rising to meet the steady horn filling her ears.

Above it all, animals cried, mourning. The musical of the accident hadn't included Sloane.

Yellow flashed in her spotted vision. Rubbing at her eyes burned, as a weeping wound dripped blood into them.

Glass cut into her knees and stabbed into her hands as she crawled through the remnants of a bumper and bits of brush. Francesca screamed Sloane's name, but through cotton-stuffed ears, she heard no reply. A broken horn in a crushed car with useless seat belts could have drowned her out. Francesca rose on shaky legs and propelled herself towards the passenger side.

Still and nearly covered by fractured trees, Francesca found Sloane covered in lacerations. Parts of her were twisted outside where they should have been in. She shouldn't be seen so, so exposed. Francesca tried to put everything right again and not to cry as she saw leaves mix in. Despite the cacophony around her, Francesca's world had gone silent.

Turning Sloane on her side, Francesca fitted herself in the crook of Sloane's body–always the little spoon. She intertwined Sloane's mangled fingers with her own and wrapped Sloane's limp, tattooed arm around her weak, bare ones. As her lace dress soaked with Sloane's warmth, Francesca stopped existing.

When flashing lights arrived, hands pulled Francesca away from Sloane. She screamed as carefully packed organs fell out in a horrific tableau.

The responders shivered.

Sloane

A FOG-LIKE EXHAUST SURROUNDED HER, suffocating.

There had been no time to mourn for herself, as fear for Francesca had taken hold. Sloane stood by her as Francesca had done the unthinkable and re-stuffed Sloane as if she were an old ratty toy whose stitching had come loose.

Horrified, they grieved together but worlds apart.

Sloane tried to follow as they whisked a broken Francesca and Sloane's gory body away. She only remembered taking one step before being sucked through the mists and dropped in her living room as if she'd meant to be there all along. Heartbroken, Sloane sat and stood, stood and sat–listless, alone, gone.

Francesca came days later, mute and swollen.

Each night she tossed and turned in Sloane's pajamas on Sloane's side of the bed. Francesca tried to avoid sleep, just crying and breathing, but spiteful exhaustion claimed her nightly. Morning waves of grief made it easy to keep track of days.

FRANCESCA

After

S he leaned in. "It's okay to talk about her."

Francesca's third therapist since her brief hospital stay sat in a two-piece Easter-egg pink business suit. An uncomfortable looking armchair framed her, making her appear small and insignificant, which wasn't too far off. Francesca chose her at random in search of a less talkative head who wouldn't start each session with, "It's okay to talk about her".

Was that the reason she'd come? Or had she come to stare at another stranger and wonder, 'Why her'?

Francesca stayed silent. Her potential new therapist, Jessica, readjusted her ankles.

Out of place for her outfit and the environment, shiny onyx stilettos squeaked as they brushed each other. Francesca pictured Jessica in a corset and not much else, standing on some man's chest, shouting at him, whip in hand.

"Why don't we start with something smaller?" What could that be? Perhaps the day's events? "How was your day?"

Sighing, Francesca muttered, "Well, my boss finally gave up on me." Not that she blamed him. She shouldn't have hit the fuck-you button when he'd called to ask her when she'd finally show up to work.

He'd given her months off, but the one day she'd made it into work, she'd fallen apart. The smell of the burnt coffee had reminded her of griping to Sloane when she'd come home every night. Francesca had tried work since; she'd even driven to the office once and sat in the parking lot. She'd chosen a grey day–a mistake. Pounding rain had felt like an invitation to sob. Her tears, her shaking body, were hidden by the thick drops smearing grey across her windshield. When she could breathe again, Francesca had driven away knowing she'd never work there again. Still, she hadn't had the energy to tell him she quit.

Useless Jessica nodded. Making odd noises, she scribbled furiously as though Francesca had said something terribly interesting and insightful.

She stuck her pink glossed lips out. "So, how does that make you feel?"

"You're kidding right?"

With a questioning look, Jessica said, "No."

That ended Jessica's short-lived life as her therapist.

She sputtered and waved her hands helplessly as Francesca abruptly stood and left her boxy room filled with decoupaged tissues boxes and calming posters made for dentists' offices.

"We could–" she began. An overly heavy door slammed on her sentiment.

As if her mother had psychic abilities, Francesca's phone rang before she reached her car.

"Hold on," she answered, annoyed. She almost hadn't picked up, but she'd ignored two of her calls in the last week due to her inability to speak through hiccuping sobs, so she owed her at least one conversation.

With her mother on speaker in her lap, Francesca felt it safe to start talking. "Hi Mama, what's up?"

"How was your appointment?"

"Well, technically I should still be in it, so you tell me."

A string of syllables crackled through Francesca's cell phone. Full sentences were lost, but her mother's concern about her adding another mark on her psychiatric belt came through crystal clear. Francesca's phone hung up on Mama, saying what she wouldn't.

When she'd made it out of the parking garage and onto the highway, heading towards home, she called Mama back.

"Parking garages, am I right? I could barely hear you, but I get it."

"Do you?" Italian flew over the line. "We've gone over this, Essie. How many is that now? Four? Five?"

Three, actually. If Francesca hadn't felt like a week old balloon, she would have corrected her. Three wasn't terrible. They were not dissimilar to shoes; she couldn't just go with the first one she tried on. There were hundreds of pairs at hundreds of stores within a few miles drive.

"I just want to go home."

"Oh, Essie! I'm so glad to hear it. I'll make a bed for you now. When do you want to leave? I'll pay for the ticket, but it should be one way, no need to plan when you go back. Maybe you don't? Pack light. We'll shop when you arrive; it'll be like a whole new start!" her mother exclaimed so rapidly, the entire conversation might as well have been on an episode of the Italian Gilmore Girls.

Mama hung up the phone before she could respond, or think, or breathe. What just happened?

A horn honked somewhere close, and her heart stopped. Francesca slammed on her brakes so quickly the seatbelt bit into her chest.

Screeching tires, yells, and slamming doors followed more horns. Francesca looked up to realize nothing horrible had happened; another angry driver had gone berserk about who-knew-what. She had almost created a pile-up on the Southern Embarcadero Highway.

Maybe Mama had been right, she needed another break–not forever, but for a little while.

The gas pedal seemed to press itself to carry her away from the angry mob.

Worried someone would have called the police on the crazy woman who brakes for ghosts, Francesca took back roads from then on. Luckily, she hadn't been far from home. She only had seven anxiety-laden turns, four heart-pounding stop signs–one of which had a police officer who had looked at her little blue bug sideways with its half scraped away sign–and six irritating pedestrians in her way.

When The Dick had called her earlier in the day, she'd had a feeling her car would need a new paint job.

"Um, Francesca," he'd stuttered. "I've tried to be patient, you know? But I call, and you don't pick up. Don't say anything..." She had no intentions. "I've just got to say this. You're... you're fired. We can't have unreliab–"

"Okay. I'll come pick up my stuff later." As Francesca hung up, she'd known she wouldn't. She'd strolled outside with an ice scraper–something Sloane made fun of her for having–and started scratching. Some of the letters peeled away smoothly, while others took the royal blue car paint with them. They'd left only the silver metal frame with jagged scrape marks. After an hour, she'd given up; what remained read, ' rli 's v Pl n g . t us h w k fo you. Call us now at (8 0) 5 3- 0 89'. Charlie would love it.

Street parking had always been horrible. On any no-good-very-bad day, it became especially awful. She had to park at least three blocks away from their shoebox above a bead store.

It had been a mistake to wear Sloane's favorite flats; they were one size too small. Blisters formed by the time she arrived at a front door they'd painted so many times rainbow chunks peeled off when it moved. Their landlord never minded what they did, because they were going to stay there until they were old and wrinkled. Never grey, Sloane had always said.

"They make hair dye for that. Silver or purple, maybe, but never grey."

SLOANE

A shadow flickered in the room's corner keeping her from spiraling further by focusing on the past months. Sloane whipped her head to the right. Was it a trick of the light? Their house phone honked, interrupting yet another thought.

Francesca stared at the answering machine in vague anticipation. A familiar woman's voice rattled off Italian.

Sloane remembered hearing it for the first time and wishing she'd had subtitles. Mama Nuccio only visited once a year—if they were lucky—still, she'd insisted on learning. No matter which language Mama Nuccio wanted to use in person or on the phone, she'd understand it. For the next two years, Sloane had learned and relearned bits and pieces of Italian. Her brain hadn't been able to grasp any foreign language until Francesca.

"You can do this; you've just got to stop and breathe. You're getting too stressed about the tenses. It's not as hard as you're making it out to be, love." Francesca had giggled at Sloane's frustration one evening. "Let's play our game, see if that can't de-stress you a little. Or was that your plan all along?"

Maybe. Sloane loved Francesca's hands-on style of teaching, what could she say?

"If you think it will help, Teach," Sloane replied. She'd jumped onto the bed and tried not to shiver.

Francesca had straddled Sloane and spoken slowly as she pulled off her tank top. Each time Sloane repeated the word or phrase incorrectly, Francesca would slide the shirt back on excruciatingly slowly.

However, when her Italian pronunciation had passed the grade, Sloane had loved the pleasure of hearing the hooks of her bra snap and feeling the band release from around her. Francesca's lips, hands, teeth hadn't touched her until they'd finished the entire lesson. By then, Sloane had lain on her back naked with the windows still wide open.

Some nights they'd touched and teased until stars collided. Others, it was fast, hard, and parades two blocks away could hear them.

Nights like those allowed Sloane to understand most of what Mama Nuccio's message said.

"The plane leaves at 5:30. It will cost a lot of money to change, so don't be late. Okay? It's for the best, Essie," she said, calling Francesca by her term of endearment. "Sloane would want this for you. You know that."

Wait!

What did she mean? Was Francesca leaving?

No, Sloane wouldn't want that for Francesca! She'd want Francesca to stay in their home until they were old and purple–never grey–just as they had planned. It would give Sloane the time she needed; she hadn't accomplished anything.

"You don't know what Sloane would want," Francesca whined softly towards the machine.

Hunched shoulders and a drooping head kept her still at

first. Eventually, with a heave, she picked up her head and pushed the blanket aside. Atrophied calves shook as she stood.

Floating around the house, Sloane tried to halt her packing process. She tried again to knock over the knock-off Tiffany lamp they'd bought at an antique show in San Mateo. As her hand passed right through it, she cursed. Almost eleven months and she hadn't figured it out.

She attempted to indent a pillow with an angry fist; her tattoos looked like one black sleeve as she tensed her arm. After failing to rattle a bowl filled with sour milk and a food-crusted spoon, she tried to grab things from Francesca's hand. But Sloane knew she could only watch in abject horror.

Francesca's eyes were too busy swimming to choose logical items. She grabbed a hodgepodge of clothing, a hairbrush, a toothbrush that she forgot to use regularly as of late—much to Sloane's nonverbal attempts to remind her, the book she wasn't reading, and a myriad of Sloane's things. One of Sloane's favorite worn t-shirts made it in before Francesca remembered deodorant.

The entire contents of Sloane's side table were tossed into her bag: two zebra gum wrappers from the afternoon Francesca had taken her to Toys-R-Us to have a real childhood experience, a ripped notebook paper that read, "Sloane, You're my forever," an old book that smelled like wonder, and a chipped coffee mug with a purple lipstick stain.

Sloane's perfume was collected last, seemingly so it could be on top. Though Sloane watched Francesca untwist the glass strawberry day after day, she never sprayed it. Francesca tugged a cotton candy pink crop-top sweater with sparkles woven through it from atop one of the many stacks of books which made up their library loft of an apartment. Carefully she rolled the frosted pink glass strawberry bottle in the rayon cotton blend.

Francesca buried her face in the sweater. After a moment, she pulled back and sobbed.

"Now you've gone and ruined it! It can never smell like her again. And you've stained it. Everything is your fault, Francesca. You did this; you caused everything. You kil–"

Her voice dropped to a whisper as she apologized to Sloane once again. Abandoning her packing, she crawled into bed and wrapped her limbs around one of Sloane's many salt and drool crusted pillows. Her chest caved in with the loss of Sloane who stood by the bed begging to be heard. When a shadow flickered in her peripheral again, she didn't turn. All the while, Sloane willed Francesca to feel the hand hovering over hers.

An annoying techno song sounded Francesca's alarm in the morning, and Sloane tried to scream through the encompassing mist. "I'm here, don't go." Still, no words came out. Her lip quivered. "What if I can't leave?"

After her morning ritual of remembering the accident, Francesca grabbed her suitcase and glanced around the room through blurred vision. Without brushing her hair or teeth, Francesca left Sloane to stare at a closing door. The lock's soft click trapped her in her own home.

Sloane wanted to drug herself to sleep, forget it all, not notice the time Francesca was gone. But no matter how many times she closed her eyes, they'd always creak back open–her body wide awake despite her mind's fogginess matching The Gray's.

Sloane could never have another second of Francesca's love. At least Francesca experienced it in her dreams; whether that made it better or worse, Sloane wished she could see for herself. Instead, her chest ached with the loss and absence.

Book stacks that used to comfort Sloane closed in on her. Dirty dishes sat in the sink. Her imagination of the odor through The Gray made her gag. Dust clumps clung to the velvet backs of face down framed photographs of her and Francesca. Months without cleaning left their house a shell of the lively home it once had been. And now, Sloane would be stuck in the lifeless home alone.

Straddling the line of devastation and rage, she watched the light change through their single picture window. Francesca was so present in the tiny loft that Sloane began to resent her for renting them the hole-in-the-wall she'd wanted.

When they'd first moved in together, neither of them had known how to exist in a small space with another person, despite Francesca having lived with friends and other lovers. They couldn't seem to stop bumping into one another, saying, "Excuse me," like strangers. After over a week of awkward days and steamy nights, Francesca's shoulder had nearly touched Sloane's as she left the bathroom. Sloane had grabbed and kissed Francesca before she could apologize for being in the same space.

"I never want to hear you apologize or say, 'Excuse me,' again unless I've got a paintbrush in my hand and paint gets on something it shouldn't. Got it?" In an attempt to look serious, she'd pulled her invisible eyebrows together.

Francesca had hugged Sloane tightly. "I promise to kiss you instead of saying anything. How's that?"

"That–" Her smile had widened. "I can work with."

Sloane stared at a miniature card from Francesca's great-grandmother she'd thumbtacked to the side of a bookshelf. A mouse in overalls sat in a teacup. Inside, squiggly handwriting told her she was a beautiful and sweet girl. As if a beacon cutting through The Gray, it was a sign that she'd have to come home.

Did Francesca leave to forget about Sloane? Months of pain

and grief, and she had to be done? If Sloane found a way to Italy, found a way to see Francesca again, would it matter?

She couldn't touch her. Francesca could barely sense her. But Sloane probably shouldn't go anywhere. Francesca couldn't live without that card.

Another flicker of darkness interrupted Sloane's spiral. She turned only to see a dirty kitchen slightly obscured by mist.

"What's going on?" she shouted to an empty room—each syllable snatched by The Gray almost as fast as they escaped her lips.

The only sounds were the tink of the water from the boiler room hitting copper pipes and the songs of traffic as they leaked through the broken window seal above Francesca's side of the bed. Silent to the world, Sloane sighed. The ambient noise their home had provided lulled Sloane to sleep, inspired her paintings, become the soundtrack of her lovemaking—it had been everything.

She'd leave and never hear it again, forget it existed even, just to see Francesca's freckles again.

FRANCESCA

The man beside Francesca coughed loudly and nudged her elbow off the armrest. "Excuse me; sorry," he mumbled as he settled into the stiff, blue cushioned scat beside her.

"Sure, my arm wasn't there," she mumbled to the middle-aged, overweight man in a suit. Angry rap pumped from his headphones. Either he was deaf or in pain.

Lights dimmed, and cold, plastic air burst through tentacle vents overhead. Francesca wanted to sleep through as many of the nineteen hours that lay ahead of her as humanly possible.

Her second therapist had been a psychiatrist, so he thought pills were better than talking. The useless three sessions had begun the same, but he'd given her Eszopiclone for her nightmares.

After she had filled the prescription, she'd never seen Dr. You-Have-Twelve-Disorders again. She had a few chalky white pills left; they still resided in a small clamshell box in her purse. Due to the fact she wouldn't have to get off the plane for any stops it made, she almost took one. But a look around at the passengers had her thinking better of it. Earbuds would have to do. Francesca got uncomfortable, and the plane took off.

An unhappy baby screamed as her ears popped. "Please remain seated–" A squeaky drawl droned over a crackling system. "Until the seatbelt light–"

Francesca had picked a winner of a flight. Only fifteen feet away from the attendant and her walky-talky couldn't project her voice seven rows back.

Why had she agreed to go to Italy again? She'd stopped crying publicly altogether. No one needed to know about the nights. Or God, the mornings. Eventually, she would be able to function an entire day without crying at all; she would work on saving it all for the nights. Those may be bad forever.

Before she knew it, a woman made her way down the cramped aisle with a little metal cart, squeezing a release handle to make it roll. It was reminiscent of the horrible wheelchairs some hospitals have that discourage anyone from actually using them; they basically have a sign which reads, 'Use at your own risk. Pusher may break fingers, and rider may end up with a spinal cord injury'.

"Water? Coffee? Coke? Orange Juice? A little something *extra*?" The flight attendant's muddled brown eyes filled with a combination of pity and worry. A dare lived behind it. 'I dare you to get drunk at 8:30 in the morning. Be that person.'

Francesca slid her earbuds out. Her throat felt rawer than usual as she croaked, "Water, coffee, and do you have Irish cream?" She didn't want it, but ruffling feathers sounded entertaining.

"Yes, uh, one second. I have to–"

The harried woman scrambled back to the curtained area of the plane. When she came back, frazzled with a side of irritated, she held the bottle with a look of distaste. "Sorry, I forgot to restock the cart. I usually do that before dinner."

Jab noted.

"Cream? Sugar?" Dishwater blonde hair was pulled up in a frizzy bun. Last night must have been a rough one for her too—only she'd probably had more fun.

Could she have more questions?

"Extra napkins?"

Of course.

"Cream and extra napkins would be great, thanks." Francesca hoped she sounded pleasant; she didn't feel pleasant.

A bit of black covered the woman's canine tooth. Whether food or decay, Francesca didn't comment on it.

"A'course darling. Let me know if you need anything else." The fake smile revealed two other places where specks clung to her teeth. She could use a brush.

The instant coffee tasted like dirt. It reminded Francesca of playgrounds, swings, the first time she'd pushed Sloane so high she'd squealed, "This is amazing! It's like I'm flying." Francesca had been so happy, and yet so sad at that. Her tear ducts burned like fire.

Maybe 'a little something extra' wouldn't be the worst thing. It was going to be a long flight.

Stuffing her earbuds in, she turned the music up to eleven. The bottle of 'extra' was small; she drank it down in one gulp. In an hour, she'd probably want another. No, maybe it wasn't the worst thing at all.

Every so often, a hairy arm would tap on her shoulder to ask her about herself, to which she gave short, quipped answers.

"Where ya headed?" Cologne and stale breath hit Francesca at the same time.

Ha. What a conversation starter: 'Are you on the same long flight to the same international destination as me?'

Even if she'd had another flight planned for after, she wouldn't be telling a stranger about it.

"Livingston, Nevada." Was that a place?

"What do you do for a living?"

"Got laid off."

Fifteen minutes later, just as Francesca had begun to doze off, the rotund man bothered her once again. "Oh, how rude! I totally forgot to ask your name, mine's Cory."

"Charlotte." A woman's got to lie now and again.

"What kinds of things do you like to do?" he asked, leaning into her.

Francesca pressed as far back into her seat as she could. "I hate most things."

Cory stopped talking to her for a long while. Almost an hour, a nice nap, and two angry girl jams later, he tapped her again.

"Are you married?"

After glancing at her bare finger, she burst into silent tears. Cory turned away and curled into an in-flight pillow.

TwENTY-THREE HOURS LATER, Cory stretched sweaty arms forward nearly punching Francesca. "What a flight!"

It was indeed.

Francesca's swollen cheeks probably looked covered in splattered burst blood vessels, not freckles. Sloane had loved how unusual it was for the Italian to be covered, while the sort-of Irish only had three moles on her entire body. They made a beautiful triangle Francesca had loved to trace on the underside of her left breast.

The plane had a semi-orderly line of people waiting to grab their bags from overhead and go on their way. Most seemed to be on vacation. When Francesca stopped to think about what she'd packed, it overwhelmed her.

A blank spot lived where the memory of her putting items in

her suitcase should have been. Had she packed her favorite necklace?

Her fingers flew up to her neck. She sighed and leaned against the side of the polyester material–still on. Sloane had given her a key at the end of their second date. Before Francesca had crawled into bed that night, she'd hung it from the only free chain she'd had–a cheap and ugly thing that had eventually turned her neck green. After they'd replaced the chain, she'd occasionally forget to put it on in the morning. Guilt sawed at her for being forgetful.

Her purse always had headphones, her wallet, passport–much to Sloane's and her mother's worry–and gum. She popped some into her gummy mouth.

Sloane's possessions had come with her, which was a relief. Which possessions, however, were all wrong. Francesca wanted more: the dresses they'd worn at their commitment ceremony, the five rings Sloane used to wear, her bracelet, Sloane.

She broke away from her darkening thoughts. At least she'd remembered the perfume. Francesca enjoyed imagining the Strawberry Fields still clung to Sloane's favorite pink sweater. It didn't.

Like a scratch-and-sniff, it had dried up months ago. But Francesca didn't want to waste a drop by spraying it on the sweater again. Maybe being rolled up together would re-invigorate the smell.

Francesca shifted from one foot to the other. She wouldn't mind being off the plane.

Cory seemed unperturbed and as chatty as ever. Ignoring him turned out to be more difficult than expected, but imagining him as a chubby bee from a children's play helped immensely. His headband antennae smacked the top of the cramped plane; his wings hooked on the chairs. Sloane would have appreciated the imagery.

In desperate need of a good crack and massage, her back ached. Sloane had been the only one who'd ever been able to get the one knot under her shoulder blade out. Francesca's breath caught again. She wiggled her nose and rolled her eyes upward.

As she pulled her purple duffle bag from the overhead compartment, she wondered again if she'd made a colossal mistake. In the five minutes following that thought, logistics began to set in.

The apartment! Francesca had to call and pay her landlord, Timothy, a month in advance so it would still be there. She'd be back. Wouldn't she? Their life was there. Sloane's smell, her laughter; everything would be lost if Francesca didn't go home.

Was the airport an acceptable place to leave a car for an untold amount of time?

Finally, she trudged down the aisle towards fresh air and her smothering mother on weak muscles. She spent most of the trek to the baggage area practicing a smile. But the moment she saw Mama waving a silk scarf she'd had since dinosaurs had roamed the earth, Francesca dropped her bags and ran. Crouching into Mama's small arms, she sobbed.

DOZING ON A LARGE STONE PATIO, Francesca stared out at an expansive valley and tried to shake off jet lag.

The too-white cushions were so plush, it was easy to forget almost anything but the view for a while. Mama owned a villa in Montepulciano, a little over two hours away from the Pisa airport. Francesca had not visited her yet. It had been in Sloane's three-year plan. Several things had been.

"Wake up." Mama broke through another windy road of Sloane. "You've been sleeping too long," she spoke in English. As

Mama rarely spoke anything but Italian, using it was probably to make Francesca feel more comfortable.

They'd used both languages when Francesca was a child. However, when Mama had moved back to Italy, she'd stopped speaking English almost entirely. She enjoyed pretending to be the cute, fumbling little Italian woman who tried her best to speak other languages; that was hardly the case as Mama had learned to speak French and German fluently while they lived in New Mexico–nearly all of Francesca's childhood. Mama tried to learn multiple different Native American languages as well, but none of those took.

"It's fine, Mama. We can speak in Italian," Francesca assured her. Obligatorily, her lips curved up into what she hoped was a smile.

Mama's small shoulders drooped. "Thank goodness, Essie. I tell you, I'm not great at English anymore. I am good at cooking," she joked as she brought the subject back to why she had come outside in the first place. Aged hands, shades tanner than Francesca, held a large black tray as if she were a server. "Here, eat." Italians.

When Mama dropped the four plates of pasta in front of her on the wrought iron patio table, she beamed. A curl fell into her eye, but the wind made quick work of it. The wine bottle patterned apron Francesca had bought her for her birthday flew up. Mama pushed it down; her small hands slid over stains of cream and red near the pockets.

"Why aren't you eating?"

"You just sat it down. Oh, and I'm not hungry."

Her mother's eyes narrowed as her thick brows clenched together. "You're too skinny. Susan liked your curves. Eat, for her."

"Sloane," Francesca corrected but nodded.

Worrying with a string on the seam of her grey tank top, she stared at nails which used to be long and manicured. Sloane used to make fun of her for her obsession with them. Without her joking mockery, Francesca had bitten them to the quick and skinned the sides pink. She'd gotten her first pimple since middle school two months ago, and her hair fell limp–an extraordinary loss.

Everything about Francesca had lost its luster.

She and Sloane had first met in a grocery store checkout line. It had been through an off-the-cuff compliment about the natural black curls that hung down to the middle of her back. Francesca could still feel Sloane's hand graze the small of her back.

If she hadn't already believed in love at first sight, when their eyes met, she'd have changed her tune.

Francesca had almost blurted, "I love you," right then and there.

Then, the world had faded away, until only Francesca and a woman with porcelain skin, fiery hair, and pouty lips had remained.

"You have beautiful hair," Sloane'd said. Her own striking Irish red curls had been in a messy loop at the top of her head, bits of fuzz and baby hairs sticking out every which way. "I have always wanted hair like that, not this–" She'd wrinkled her forehead to look up and tug at a stray curl, cursing as it frizzed. Her white-blonde eyebrows had wriggled in a way Francesca would come to rely on to tell her how Sloane felt. "Mess."

She'd turned to go, a barely filled paper bag in hand, but Francesca never wanted her to leave.

"Wait. Can I–I mean, are you...?" She'd looked straight into Sloane's emerald eyes and composed herself. "Would you be interested in having coffee with me?"

Sloane had laughed and shaken her head, bringing a flare to

Francesca's cheek, though her olive skin covered most of it. "Funny."

"Oh." Francesca had wished she could leave. "It's fine."

As if she'd been waiting for a punchline, Sloane's red eyelashes blinked a few times. "No, I laughed because I thought you were kidding."

"Can you two lovebirds move it along?" A woman in a jogging suit had tapped her foot. "I have ice cream in the cart, and my kid's soccer practice is over at 6:30. I really wanted to have a nice soak and sneak a few glasses of wine in before I have to pick him up."

Francesca had tried to keep the grin off of her face before she swiveled back to Sloane. "Now? Later? Both?"

Though she'd turned down offers to dinner from two men and a woman only days ago, she'd sounded as though she couldn't get a date. Great. To top it off, her cart had been full of cat-lady style foods: frozen dinner meals, instant foods, poppable fruits, and–to her horror–jarred pasta sauce.

Sloane's face had lit up. "Both."

Francesca had fallen in love. And they still hadn't introduced themselves.

A cool breeze brought the scent of Mama's red wine lamb tomato sauce into focus. It reminded her she wasn't standing under unflattering bright light beside movie candy and batteries. The gut-punch that her Sloane wasn't there followed seconds later.

To top it off, Mama's slant on bolognese had been Sloane's favorite. Francesca shoveled the cooling pasta in without tasting it, feeling sicker with each bite. Her heart mimicked each tomato as they burst into her mouth. Their insides still felt like lava; Francesca could relate.

She couldn't escape the memories, even in Italy.

Sloane's ghost was ever present, sitting beside her, clinging.

Francesca let herself imagine a translucent Sloane waving at her.

"Hey baby, sorry it took me so long to make contact. Being a ghost sucks. Do you think we'll be able to make this whole dead thing work, you know like Patrick Swayze and Demi what's-her-last-name-now?"

She'd say it exactly like that. Francesca's smile was genuine as she started to vomit.

~

"O Dio Mio!"

Warm wind blew through an arched stone window. Francesca lay on a king-sized bed with five linen duvets in an ombre of dark grey to white surrounded by a mound of pillows. She waved Mama's shouts off, hoping her arm could be seen from within the comfy cave she'd hidden in.

Francesca had taken a quick shower, paying close attention to the areas in her hair where vomit had clung. Wet strands cut into her eyes as she tried to turn.

"O' way," muffled through the fabric.

"You got sick, Essie. All over the patio."

Kudos, Mama had such insight. Francesca almost mouthed off but was still suffocating herself. She began the process of rolling over.

"Are you more worried about me or the patio?" she asked when she could breathe again.

Mama bristled.

Sitting up felt as though Francesca were underwater. She fully faced her small-framed mother who's hips barely breached the height of the pillow top mattress.

"I'm sorry, Mama. I know you just don't want your patio to get dirty." She tried to crack a smile, failed, and gave into one of the sighs that had been looming in the back of her throat since she'd agreed to get on the plane.

"Essie, my darling," Mama said, as she scrambled onto the bed. Even when she looked tiny, Francesca's mother was a glamorous woman. "Start from wherever you need to."

Mama's hand felt cool and clammy on Francesca's.

"I–Her name is Sloane, not Susan," she murmured, still hung up on Mama's slip up. "Okay?" Francesca nodded for Mama.

That was all she'd say on Sloane for the evening–though it was barely the afternoon. The time to shatter was upon her.

IT MUST HAVE BEEN the next morning, nearly an entire day later, when Francesca awoke to the smell of cinnamon rolls and the usual sickness as she remembered the car accident in slow motion.

Heat prickled her eyes as she curled up in a ball. She clenched her fists and calmed herself second by second; those were how she marked her progress. She considered one less second of pain a success.

By the time she could process the current day, she was transported to another morning of cinnamon rolls and sadness.

Warm icing had dripped from her finger as she'd gone to lick it off. Francesca hadn't left the bed in two days, tears and drool crusted in small circles on her pillow like chicken pox.

Kevin had broken up with her. She'd cried, not for the loss of a decent boyfriend, but because she'd had to tell her mother she was gay. As she'd bitten into the barely cooked dough, the words had come out. Muffled, she'd told Mama what she had assumed would be a shock.

Nodding, her mother had said, "Yes, yes. Another roll?" Oh.

A neighbor had come by later that day.

Francesca remembered Mama being so proud to tell him Francesca had finally admitted it; they'd clinked tea glasses.

Francesca should have gone to Japan. She didn't have as many associations with it. But sushi would probably remind her of Sloane. They had also discussed at length the difference in clothing styles once, getting into a heated argument over the difference in lolita fashions. It had ended in an internet shopping spree. Mexico would remind her of their annual Día de Los Muertos party. Germany, Romania, Ireland, and anything in between, around, near, or far was out, too. They'd planned a year-long trip to Europe. There wasn't a place she could think of where she could escape. Her breath hitched.

A metal show at full capacity with deep bass thumped too loudly inside of her head–a feeling to which she'd become accustomed. Her jaw popped, as she called out to Mama. "What's that I smell?"

The door to her temporary bedroom swung open. Mama swooped in carrying a blue and white flower printed plate overflowing with cinnamon pastries smothered with liquid sugar.

"Eat," Mama instructed. Francesca appreciated her lack of comment on the dried snot decorating the front of her t-shirt and pillow. "Your body is empty," she said with a pointed look. "So, you need something."

"And sweets is what you chose? Not that I'm complaining." Francesca added, the roll already on its way to her mouth. Mama had good ideas once in a while. "Thank you for yest–"

"Hush. Another roll?" Francesca hadn't finished the first one. "When you finish, we'll go shopping."

Francesca smiled and coughed the first one down. "That was a bigger bite than I was expecting. Mama, you don't have to take me shopping."

She'd eaten half the next roll before Mama responded.

"We've talked about this. You came with next to nothing, and

I saw what you brought: pieces of different seasons wardrobes and random trinkets. Not much in there that will work for the heat. So we're going shopping. I'm going to buy you some new things. It's good to have a fresh start. Sloane would want that."

'You don't know what Sloane would want!' Francesca nearly shouted out loud. Her mother seemed to know Sloane pretty well whenever it suited her needs.

Instead of starting a fight, Francesca nodded. "You're right; I need new things. I don't have much to wear. Besides, I haven't seen any part of Italy since we visited when I was, what... fourteen?" Licking her lips, she sweetly told Mama to get out so she could get ready.

When the door closed behind her, Francesca made no move to untangle herself from her fluffy cocoon.

A bell chimed off into the distance. Seven rings seven a.m. No wonder she felt so grumpy and tired.

Her body shouted at her; she should be getting ready for bed, or maybe she'd already be tucked in—even after almost seventeen hours of sleep. Eleven months ago, she and Sloane would have been in their pajamas reading to each other. The sound of the city bell may cause her a lot of problems.

"Ready?" Mama's voice came through the open window. She had gone outside to pick fresh flowers.

Francesca decided not to answer, as she still hadn't started the process of getting out of the bed. Mama's humming was an ocean view; it comforted and grounded her as it reminded her she was only a mere speck in the world. Francesca never understood how a soft sound could do so much. Maybe it was the tune—something she could never place, but would never forget.

As it was one of maybe three outfits that made sense, she chose a white sundress and silver sandals for the early morning shopping day. It felt a little more Greek-vacation than Italian-life.

Francesca only owned three pairs of shoes, of which she'd brought two. Her bag also revealed the one dress, one pair each of jeans and shorts, four tee shirts, and a bulky sweater. Besides her small wardrobe and the outfit she wore on the plane–the pajama pants she wore to bed each night, a tank top, and a jean jacket–she had enough underwear and socks for one week.

Damn. Her mother was right; she needed to go shopping.

At least Sloane's perfume had made it.

The flat cork soles of her sandals loudly flapped as she made her way out to the garden. Her mother was bent over collecting lavender.

"My, don't you look stunning? That's a nice outfit!" A pause. "Oh! I didn't even see the sandals–very cute, Es. How many did you bring? But, look how pale you are! Your freckles are like stars, so bright!"

Francesca had become so used to being compared to her fair-skinned Sloane she'd forgotten she was pale for an Italian.

"Mama, you know I don't go out much. But Sloane and I got plenty of vitamin D. And why is it bad that you can see my freckles? It's what makes me such a special Italian."

Francesca laughed at her comment, then smiled at the flashes that popped into her head: long car rides with candy wrappers filling the floorboards; cold, out-of-the-way waterfalls; filtered light streaming through high tree branches–branches that killed Sloane. Her eyes watered–every memory destroyed.

"Why the tears, my Essie?"

She did not want a heart-to-heart.

"Let's just go shopping."

THE NARROW ROAD laid in front of them, winding like a vein. Francesca's mood had her sinking into a dark place.

She'd claw her way out of it, Mama said, as they drove to Sienna: "A good spot to shop."

During the fifty minute drive, the blue sky said, "Please smile."

Puffy clouds shaped themselves into magical animals that had Francesca wanting to call them out as she did when she was a child. Fields of flowers and grassy pastures were set to vivid, as their colors came alive. Fresh scents followed, begging her to give in to the beautiful day.

The warm air pleaded with her. "Just toss your head back. You're in a convertible, for goodness sakes."

In truth, it had been her mother who had said it all. But caught up in the scenery and sensations, they felt more concrete to Francesca than her sweet Mama.

Her hair whipped quickly and painfully around her face. Mama pointed to the glove box where a stack of scarves resided on the usual important paperwork and a mother-of-pearl flask.

Francesca fumbled as she attempted to wrap a large square of yellow-flowered white silk around her head. Her failure knotted the fabric and added a layer of nuisance.

"Show me later," she said. Francesca had not mentioned the flask. Too cute, her mother.

When they'd pulled into a nearly empty row of parking spots, Mama showed her how to use the scarf. But the moment she finished tying the knot, Francesca forgot what she'd just learned. Looking sleek and sophisticated with her new wrap, Francesca wore a smile for Mama as they walked through a glass door with a scrawled etching that read 'Marta's Boutique.'

"See? Beautiful, no? It's been ages since you've visited Sienna. You may not remember much except for photos. We're near the Piazza del Campo; that's our next stop."

Francesca couldn't recall going into the store, or picking out clothes; she may not have.

Still, she waited in a small changing room in her cream and white polka-dotted underwear and a warped off-white bra for another item of clothing to be handed to her over the door. Apparently, she wasn't to be trusted with them all at once.

Modeling each item seemed imperative.

Why? Because she wasn't trusted to pick out her wardrobe, that's why. Mama and the shop owner, Marta, did.

The first dress she tried on was impractical, long, blue chiffon. They loved it. Francesca only wanted a few nice shirts, a few pairs of shorts, a skirt or two, and one fancy dress because her mother went out to eat often.

After Francesca complained, they switched to slightly more appropriate clothing choices.

First up: a pair of jeans and a short-sleeved sweater. Impractical once again; it was hot outside, Francesca reminded them as if they were the visitors and she the resident.

"Okay, let me grab a few more pieces," Marta declared probably holding up her finger dramatically.

Her sandals squeaked as she ran around the store. Francesca could imagine Marta's round feet, which spilled out at every possible spot, gasp for air.

Tired of shopping, Francesca agreed to a few more. Possibly because they still hadn't found anything, possibly because she enjoyed the sound of metal sliding on metal as Marta found her size.

"She'll love it," Mama's voice slid under the door. "You'll love it," she finally addressed Francesca, as if just remembering she'd be the one wearing it.

It was the perfect tank top. Sloane would have picked it out for her, saying, "Francesca, it screamed you. I think the flowiness will make you happy, and red has always been your color."

And Sloane would have been right, as she usually was when she picked Francesca's clothes out.

As soon as she stepped out, ready to announce she'd finally found something, Marta clapped her hands. "Oh, Essie. You look gorgeous."

Francesca no longer cared if Sloane would have loved it. Marta had called her Essie. She was done.

"Thanks," Francesca said through tight lips. Damn. The first time in a while she'd thought of Sloane without tears, and she had to leave. "Mama, let's go. I think I need a break; I'm a bit tired. How about some lunch?"

She had no idea what time it was.

Nodding, Mama smiled. "Of course, darling." She turned to Marta. "It was such a long flight; I'm surprised she's up today at all."

Francesca did not want to be, but she didn't have much of a choice.

"We will be back later, okay Marta?" Mama said.

After Mama and Marta said many goodbyes, air-kissed, and hugged so many times Francesca lost count, they were finally off.

Mama produced a letter from her purse before the glass door banged loudly behind them and swatted Francesca; it was not the first time. "What were you thinking? Marta will think you don't like her."

"I don't think I do."

"You hush." Mama smacked her again. Francesca wondered for the billionth time if she'd ever be allowed to read that letter. She'd stopped asking when she was eleven.

There had never been a day Mama hadn't had it with her—in her purse or under her pillow. The envelope always seemed fresh and new, but never had sharp edges; when she was small, she'd convinced herself it was a magical letter holding secrets only Mamas could know.

Being swatted by that damned letter had been the only 'punishment' she'd ever known.

"Okay." Francesca nodded. She figured if her mother didn't want the truth, she didn't have to give it to her. She'd been lying for months as it was.

Francesca's sandals heels were reminiscent of hooves on the stones. *Click, clack, click, clack.* Only things that weighed a ton should make such a racket. Her mother barely seemed to notice, lost in a blissful delusion.

Francesca wondered what it would be like to be her. Men loved Mama–even when she didn't love them, her ability to pick up languages had always been first class, the only curls escaping from her perfect coif seemed to be for effect, and Mama was effortlessly beautiful. Francesca did wonder if being Mama's height might bother her.

Though an education had always been vital to her mother when it came to Francesca, she never worried about it for herself. Around intellectuals, at a gala or poetry reading–if Francesca were her mother–she may fret over every word that came out of her mouth; she may wonder if they knew or cared that she hadn't had a formal college education. As Mama, Francesca would have had a horrific divorce, causing her to question love, and a kid she had to raise on her own. It may have made her strong–strong enough to handle losing Sloane. Probably not, though.

After a too-long conversation about which pasta place Mama would take Francesca to eat, she chose Tony's–the first place she'd mentioned. The restaurant may have had another name, but her mother enjoyed name dropping when she knew anybody. It seemed she and Tony's mother, Alma Loreti, met at a wine tasting. They'd talked about ex-husbands and dating–a subject of great surprise to Francesca, as she didn't know her mother dated.

Most conversations ended up where mother's tend to, though: their children. Alma had four, but Mama only remembered Tony and Cecilia; "the other two" were off in Spain and America, so they didn't seem to warrant brain space. Though both were older than Francesca, Mama just called them The Loreti Children. She called anyone by their 'titles' if she forgot their names.

Francesca's stomach had begun grumbling at the mention of pasta, but when she smelled fresh rising yeast, her feet almost turned without her permission. Her mother smiled as she took a deep breath of the air.

"Delicious, no? Do you want to stop? I'm sure Lia has a few Zeppoles left." Is there anyone Mama doesn't know? More importantly, Zeppoles were one of Francesca's favorite desserts.

A picture window displayed baked goods stacked like Plinko pieces.

"If you insist," Francesca said. Despite her irritation, she grinned. Baked goods had that effect on her.

The sun streaked through the open door of the bakery. A shelving unit against the wall displayed various loaves of bread. Lia beamed when they came in, ready to serve her customers. Hints of lines creased around her eyes when she recognized Mama.

"Maria!" Lia came around the cement-topped counter with wide open arms. Her mint green strapless dress draped the floor. "It's been too long. And is this who I think it is? Maria, she looks just like you."

Though Lia's jet-black frizz was pinned back, it still managed to end up in Francesca's mouth as she strangled her with a hug. Francesca must have tensed, because Lia pulled back, her dark olive skin tinted pink. Francesca ignored Lia's embarrassment and thought about her own paleness again. It made her feel like a fraud of an Italian, especially with freckles that would have been more at home on Sloane's fair skin.

"Yes, it has been far too long. We mustn't let it go so long! An hour away is no excuse. And yes, yes, it is," Mama said with pride. Francesca wasn't much to be proud of at the moment: sad, alone, abandoned, angry, and–verging on–starving. "This is Francesca."

"I'm Lia. It's so very nice to meet you. I've heard so much about you. All good!" she added quickly.

Isn't that what you were supposed to say, a platitude? It wasn't as if she could tell Francesca Mama had bitched about her. And what should Francesca tell Lia when she'd heard nothing about her?

She chose: "It's nice to meet you too. I had to sneak in before lunch; it was impossible not to." She hoped her expensive teeth and compliment would make up for the lack of returned knowledge.

Lia laughed surprisingly heartily for such a slight woman. "The bread. That's its main purpose, really. I do sell it, mind you, but far less often. My regulars buy it, sure. Usually, though, people stop in because of its mouthwatering smell, and end up buying the sweets."

Francesca hated being a cliche; that hadn't stopped her before.

"I suppose we're going to follow the trend. I was hoping to grab a few Zeppoles. Mama says you make them, and in San Francisco, they only have decent ones. Please tell me you have some left?"

"I do, indeed." Lia produced a baker's dozen of Zeppoles before Francesca could decide how many she wanted–nine or ten. "Powdered sugar, I assume?"

"You assumed right." Francesca hoped Mama didn't mind paying. She hadn't remembered to exchange any of her money. Damn.

Lia more than 'dusted' the baked goodies with the cocaine

sweetener. Francesca's mouth watered, lunch forgotten. "Those look like perfection."

"They are," Lia said. "I mean, they're my grandmother's recipe, so they are heaven. I'm not bragging about myself."

"It would be okay if you were." Mama laughed. "They are the best Zeppoles in Italy." She took out her money without glancing at Francesca.

Okay, she didn't mind. That meant they could discuss it, and so many other things, over lunch.

6

SLOANE

A force pulled on her insides, tugging Sloane towards the center of the earth. Fear of the unknown struck as The Gray gripped her like an angry neighbor from her childhood. Her breath became as uneven as the ground under her. Familiar wooden slats were replaced with cobblestones. As The Gray released its hold on Sloane and ebbed back to its smoky fog, she took in her surroundings. She was in Tuscany.

Before Sloane had a moment to appreciate the sights or marvel at the fact she'd made it somehow, she heard her favorite sound.

Francesca and Mama Nuccio sat a wrought iron table laughing. She wore the sundress she'd worn during their first garden party. A friend threw a party every June where partygoers were "encouraged" to bring a homemade drink, recipe included. They'd vote on the best tasting one, best name, and most creative. Francesca preferred showing up late, so their drink would be the last the already tipsy crowd tasted–or remembered; Sloane always complained.

"What?" she'd said the first year. "You tell me about a party, and I make a plan to have us win... and you don't like it?"

"I just don't want to miss out on the tastiest drinks."

Some party-goers would bring a small pitcher that would be gone before half of the guests arrived, and Sloane hated missing fun boozy concoctions; it was the only reason she'd wanted to be so social.

Francesca had laughed. "This is the tastiest drink. Now, keep stirring, while I go change."

She'd come out in the white sundress, her hair down and wild, wearing the key necklace Sloane had given her ages before. "Ready! Let's go win us a contest!"

Seeing her in that dress again, laughing with Mama Nuccio, was like shattering glass. There were seven bags by their feet, and mounds of pasta and a carafe of white wine on the table. Mama Nuccio sparkled with energy.

Though the sun shone, a small cloud still lived around Sloane; raindrops fell on her head.

Hovering by Francesca's shoulder, Sloane shifted a napkin—no, that was the wind. Damn. Using all of the energy she had, she tried to tug on a shopping bag's thin rope handle. It wouldn't budge. Her wet cheeks almost became background noise as her lack of success made her angry, more determined. Somehow, she'd made it to Francesca, to Tuscany. She'd have to figure out what she'd done to make that happen, so she could learn to move things—a small feat, comparatively.

7

FRANCESCA

S he had to admit it; she was having fun.

Becoming used to eye-rolling half of the times her mother called—far too often, Francesca had forgotten how much she missed her.

"See, Essie? I knew you'd have fun in Italy."

The eye roll threatened to make an appearance. "I never said I wouldn't," Francesca replied. She just knew it wouldn't make Sloane's memory disappear, so she still wouldn't be okay.

Through half-chewed pasta, her mother said some joke to herself. Aloud, she said, "Ah! Here he is." She swallowed a bite so large, Francesca could see it move in her throat as if a mouse were being consumed by a snake.

"Mama Nuccio!" the tall Italian man cried joyously from inside the restaurant.

Hearing Sloane's name for her mother snatched Francesca's breath. Though it was a man's voice, she swiveled. Not Sloane, of course.

"Mama Nuccio," he began once again when he was closer. "How are you this fine afternoon? And who is this bellissimo woman? Mama Nuccio..." He raised his thick eyebrows and smirked, a dimple formed high on the right side of his cheek. He stuck his hands in the pockets of his white apron. "Is this your sister?"

Without blinking, The Letter appeared and her mother swatted him with it.

"Oh, Tony! I thought you were at your other restaurant on Saturdays. What a delight!" She laughed, and the letter disappeared into her purse. It always seemed like magic. "This is my daughter from San Francisco! She finally came to visit a frail old woman."

Tony shook all over. "Mama Nuccio, you are a lot of things, but old and frail are none of them." Long eyelashes crushed together with an over exaggerated wink.

Francesca felt like a child, as they talked about her as though she were elsewhere. But it gave her time to calm her rapid heartbeat. He spoke to Mama as Sloane had. Though her mother loved Sloane, she had given her a hard time as she had with every other person Francesca dated.

She'd always told Mama Sloane was different, but it wasn't until after the accident that she seemed to believe her.

Six years, and it appeared as though she'd still expected them to break up at any moment. As if you just "broke up" with someone after years of a committed relationship. Things wouldn't have been so cavalier. Francesca couldn't even think about a life without Sloane before she was gone. Just the thought made her eyes hot.

Mama coughed. "Francesca?"

Shoot. They had said something to her while she'd gotten lost in memories.

"Sorry, just taking in the sun. It's been too long," she said, sighing for emphasis.

They both smiled; she must have pulled it off. "Nice to meet you, Tony."

"You too, Francesca. I've heard many stories about you." His chestnut eyes took her in. "I assume they're all true, no?"

Shiny black hair was pulled back into a sleek ponytail. A slight beard grew over his full lips. He kept trying to move it as if it itched, but his smile never faltered.

"Probably. Did Mama tell you about my first spaghetti experience? She loves that one. And how I used to collect weeds instead of flowers? What about the time Sloane and I–?" Francesca broke away. Tears itched, but she recovered. "All stories I'm sure you've heard or will soon enough."

When he smiled at her, she returned a pleasant one, hoping it looked real.

"Go, go, Tony. Customers are starving, and you're to blame!" The Letter stuck out of Mama's purse. "Yes, Mama Nuccio!" He held his hands up. "Let's all have dinner soon. Mama will be so pleased you're here," he said as he turned towards Francesca.

With that, he left them alone. The mood had shifted; his presence had upset the tenuous, but happy balance.

"I'll make dinner plans for tomorrow, yes?" she asked, already pulling out a scuffed flip phone.

"You still use that thing?"

"It still works." She shrugged. A finger flew up in Francesca's face as Mama put on her phone voice. "Alma, it's Maria Nuccio."

Adding her last name made Francesca smile. The chorus to Sound of Music's "Maria" began playing in her head.

"Tony already called? So fast, that one. Yes, I was thinking tomorrow night, too." Mama bounced a little in her chair. "Mhmm. See you."

Mama pulled a notebook from her purse of wonders and began to write a list on it. "Well? It should just be a small gathering, around ten or so p–"

Francesca cut her off with an indignant, "What?"

Mama trudged on. "–At Alma's villa. What do you want to make?"

"Ten people, Mama? No, I won't do it. I can't."

It was too much, too fast. Francesca hadn't been to any gathering without Sloane in years. Though Francesca had always been the more social of the two, Sloane had her moments. The party they went to the last time Francesca wore her current outfit–something she hadn't realized until that moment–popped into her head. Her hands shook.

"What do you want to make?"

"Are you listening to me?" Francesca leaned forward.

Her eyes narrowed. "Essie, I hear you, but no I won't listen. What do you want to make?" Mama prodded.

A losing battle, Francesca hung her head. "Whatever you think is best. I may not come. We'll see."

"Sure, sure, we'll let lunch sit and pick something after we walk."

Francesca kept the 'whatever' that sat on the tip of her tongue to herself, as Mama flagged down Tony to tell him the good news. Lunch was on him, he said, adding that it was a "beautiful day for beautiful women".

They finished their wine before they wandered back into the square. Francesca hoped Mama wouldn't suggest going back to buy clothes at Marta's.

Even though she'd just finished eating, each bakery and restaurant they passed made her hungry. As they wandered into a more populated area, Francesca's shoes weren't as loud. That did wonders for her mood. Tourists stuck out, all sun-burned with fanny packs. Natives roamed, weaving through the pale visitors like a stream of olive oil. She couldn't wait until she fit that category.

At the moment, she was an "in-between": more like good

vegetable oil, a decent replacement if you were out of olive oil and didn't feel up to going to the store.

Children played ball in the small streets as if they were stuck in another time.

Francesca remembered the last time she'd seen anything like that. She and Sloane had been on a road trip to some small town with the 'World's Largest Table,' 'Largest Frying Pan,' or some other small 'Large' claim to fame. The kids had been on monkey bars, screaming about being "it." Dreamily, Sloane had sighed.

"Maybe one of those could be in our future? What do you think, love?"

Even if stars hadn't been twinkling in Sloane's jeweled eyes, Francesca still would have said yes. They hadn't had any plans beyond Sloane's question and Francesca's one-word answer. The life-changing subject had been brought up only one week before their anniversary–one week before the accident that took Sloane from Francesca, without getting the wedding Sloane wanted or the baby for which she yearned. A pang hit Francesca in two places at once.

Mama interrupted at the exact right moment. "Penny for your thoughts?"

"Sloane. I was thinking about Sloane and how we'd just started thinking about having a baby."

If she had been a few inches shorter, Francesca might not have noticed her mother's dead stop. "A what?"

"I know you weren't sure about Sloane–"

"No, Essie! I was! That's why I pushed her so hard. That's why I wanted you with me, because she was your everything love." She took a deep inhale. "And I know what it's like to lose that."

But Mama had hated her bio-dad by the end. Hadn't she?

Mama took Francesca's hand and tugged her towards a structure she recognized–if not from her childhood, from films.

The Fonte Gaia was more breathtaking than she remembered. Or maybe, as an adult, she appreciated its unique shape, expertly sculpted tableaus, and the smell of copper wishes more.

"Do you have any change?" Quiet tears streamed down Francesca's burning face, the sun drying them before they fell. Her breath hitched a little, and she clenched her fists. "Sloane always tossed a penny in to make a wish. I need all the wishes I can get right now."

Mama pulled out a quarter and a penny from the zippered pouch of her wallet. "For a small and a big wish."

Francesca's small wish was to make it through the dinner party–if she decided to go; her big wish was to make it through life without Sloane.

Tossing each coin with her right hand over her left shoulder, just as she had been taught from a young age, she took a moment to appreciate the satisfying *plop* they made when they hit the bright blue water. As they sunk to the bottom with the thousands of other coins, she wondered if any of the wishes had come true.

"Let's go home now, Mama."

BEFORE THE SKY had fully darkened, Francesca retired to her room.

Mama had grabbed Francesca's hand on her way to the back of the house. "Tomorrow is another day, Essie. Another adventure awaits."

Francesca had nodded and walked a little brisker. Relieved to hear the lock click, Francesca had slid down the door and let the evening come.

SLOANE KNEELED in front of her, ring case open. "I can't imagine spending a day without you." In one sigh, she asked, "Will you marry me?"

Francesca pulled Sloane up into her arms. As if she'd swallowed a large marble, her heartbeat throbbed in her throat. "Y–"

A loud noise broke the dream and woke Francesca, robbing her of the moment she'd never have. "Fuck."

Mama shouted to the morning, a tradition Francesca had forgotten. For once, she'd thank jet-lag; it had allowed her to sleep through Mama's noise the day before.

"Essie? Is that you?" her mother yelled. "You come out now since you're up! The door's already open."

Francesca's stomach rolled. She needed more time. Didn't Mama know Sloane's presence was missed the most in the mornings? If she didn't, Francesca couldn't explain it.

Resigned, Francesca pulled a ruffled teal skirt and a fitted white shirt from a shiny black shopping bag and shakily shouted, "I'm going to shower."

Hard droplets from the rain shower hid her morning tears, as she tried to calm herself. Just a dream–Sloane was gone, Francesca was alone, and that would be okay one day.

Toweling herself off, she ignored her sore face. One day, that too would stop being raw.

Pajamas called to her from her suitcase begging her to curl up and give in. But no, she'd come to Montepulciano for healing. Francesca laughed out loud and turned away from the mirror. Swollen freckled cheeks and red eyes would only reveal the motive Francesca hid from herself; she'd come to run away. Leaving her hair damp, she met her mother outside.

"A vision!"

Francesca smiled and tugged at a wildflower from the

nearest bush. Sticking it in her hair, she spun around. "I am, aren't I?"

She didn't actually know. She'd not gone back to the mirror.

Sloane's sparkling eyes came to mind when the fragrance of the flower wafted to Francesca's nose. Sloane picked any remotely pretty flower, even weed-like ones from sidewalk cracks, to put behind Francesca's ear. Then, they'd tango over dramatically and smooch loudly as if they were in a cartoon.

"I see the sadness behind your sarcasm. Food will help, then wine."

"It's too early for wine, Mama. I just woke up!"

She hadn't even seen her mother's purse, but before she could blink that damned letter appeared again and smacked her arm. Mama put it in a new envelope, as she did after Francesca's arm and head had bent it to limpness.

"It is never too early for wine, Essie. Now, do you want breakfast or lunch?"

"At eight a.m.? Bacon and pancakes and more cinnamon rolls, oh my!"

"Let's make it quick; some wineries open at nine am!"

NEITHER FRANCESCA nor her mother could walk in a straight line. They both swayed, and the world tilted with them. What a follow-up to breakfast, wine.

"Thiss uns the bes–tuh," Francesca declared. In her head, she said it clearly.

Mama laughed, "You slurring."

"'N you're crystal clur," she replied, hearing her letters mash together as she paid close attention to each sound.

The tour guide hadn't said anything, even as they'd gulped their fourth merlot at their third wine tour. Francesca wouldn't have cared. Slit eyes dared the slight woman in a pressed teal button-up and creased black skirt whenever she looked as though she might.

'Yes, please try and tell Mama to be quiet.' Francesca would have loved to see all 5 foot 2 of her raise up against Miss Model in heels. By the end of it, Mama would have a refund, free wine, and a voucher for another visit, along with a personal apology from the vineyard's owner.

"Another?"

"Wine or tour?" Francesca asked as her stomach demanded food, and her head demanded a jug of water.

"Both. Food first! I heard your tummy-monster."

"You've got to stop calling it that."

Flipping her long hair back, Mama smirked. "Do I? I don't think I do, because I'm your Mama. Mamas get certain privileges."

"Not when I'm an adult. Mamas get less privileges."

Mama ignored her as they wobbled out of the barrel themed tasting room. An unforgiving sun greeted them.

Francesca squinted. "I forgot it wasn't night time."

"Tonight, we have dinner with Alma."

"I forgot that too!" Francesca gasped, nerves shaking her sober-ish. "We haven't even started shopping. It took us all after-noon to end up deciding to make whatever dish you chose in the beginning. Will we make it all in time?"

Mama furrowed her brow. Francesca realized why a second later, as she navigated to open the car door.

Uh oh.

Neither of them could drive.

"We'll just sit for a bit," Francesca suggested. "Just talk, or something. How about you catch me up on what you've been up to lately?"

Snorting, Mama slid into the car. "You know these things.

What about Sloane? You haven't talked about her much."

"No." Francesca gulped. "We have dinner plans tonight. If I start crying, I may never stop."

"That's something you need to work on, Essie. Tell me a story about her, whatever you'd like to say. Something I didn't know, or maybe something I did. Your choice," Mama said.

Though they'd opened the windows, it was still a sauna. The car roared to life, and Mama cranked the air conditioning. She didn't roll her window up.

"Just for a minute," she commented. "So, tell me."

Like therapy, Francesca had the mind to clam up, storm out. But it was her mother. Sifting through the millions of stories she had on the tip of her tongue to pick just one would be hard. As if she were Mama's old car engine, she sputtered a few times as she figured it out. "Okay, well one time Sloane and I were at the park–no, I mean, we just had a picnic. We went to see A Christmas Carol, which she had never seen, and–no, that's not good enough." Hot air puffed from her nose.

"All stories are good enough, Essie," Mama said. She put her sun-spotted hand on Francesca's arm.

Francesca could breathe better. "So, a few years ago, Sloane started complaining about wanting a pillow top mattress. I didn't care one way or another–you know I can sleep standing up–but I wanted her to be happy. So, we went mattress shopping. Turns out that's a daunting process. Hours, we spent hours, testing out beds that felt the same to me. After Sloane rolled, bounced, and laid on a bed, she had something to say about each one. Goldilocks, I swear. But about everything, not just beds. It's one of the reasons I love her."

A sound of understanding came from Mama as she smiled.

"Anyhow, she was acting like a stand-up comedian; other customers noticed and started to follow us around the store to watch her critique the mattresses. We even had two couples follow us to different stores."

Francesca chuckled at her stupid story. "She'd say things like: 'If I want to wake up feeling 80-years-old in the morning, sure, this is the bed for me.' Or 'This one's *great* for anyone who's done with sex. I sink so far in, it'd be hard to do much but lay there like a dead fish–but, hey, that's a thing for some people.'"

Mama snorted at that.

"Once, she even said, 'I'm pretty sure this bed would make me pee myself. These puckers make indentions in the worst places. I'm having shooting hip pain and my bladder's scream-ing. Francesca, if you don't buy me this bed immediately, I may di–'" She cut the building laughter short. She lifted her head to face Mama. "I can't." Hot tears that had nothing to do with the weather poured down her face. "Sloane used to like my words. I think this is the most I've put together since..."

Mama's face fell with Francesca's. "That was brave, Essie. Very brave." She paused before saying, "You know, I understand this feeling. I wasn't going to say anything, but maybe it will help."

"What are you talking about, Mama?"

Mama stopped speaking Italian and switched to English as she said, "A long time ago–" Her lip quivered. "A long time ago, I lost a love. I thought he'd just never come home, but one day, I found out he was actually gone. Grief comes and goes, but it's okay to live, my *dolce*."

Between the language jolt and the secret, it took Francesca a moment to recover. And she used her childhood pet name, my dolce. Francesca's heart matched the metal show migraine she'd woken up with just two days before–all thumps, bass, and high-strung squeals.

"What?" Was that all she had? "Um, I mean, who are you

talking about? Not bio-dad, obviously. You've never told me about this lost love."

"No," she said, still speaking in English. "I don't talk about him much, because I kept thinking, 'What could I say that would make it better?' Nothing. So I just tried to avoid talking about him altogether. It didn't help, Essie."

"Is that why you haven't dated?"

The car had finally cooled to the point of chilly. Mama rolled the windows down–she must have rolled them up while Francesca chatted about Sloane.

"It's a little more complicated than that. But–" Mama wiped her welling eyes. "That's a story for another time."

"You're kidding, right? You tell me all of that, even speak in English about this guy, but now I have to wait?"

"Patience is a virtue," she crooned, then switched back to Italian. "And you should be virtuous."

"He was American, wasn't he? That's why it feels natural to talk about him in English!"

"My little detective. Later, I'll tell you more later. I feel okay enough to drive, I think. And it's about time we grab lunch and switch to a different topic."

8

SLOANE

Sloane explored the square she'd been tugged to through her rainy-day filter, but it felt hollow. With no one to share it with, seeing monuments bored her. If she could go somewhere else, more remote, she may have been okay with her aloneness.

She watched a pair of lovers so focused on each other it was as if they were alone in the crowds of tourists. The man played with the woman's hair while he whispered, "I love you." As the light began to fade, they danced by an eerily lit fountain.

Sloane's heart ached. To be in Italy and stuck once again was a cruel joke.

Nearer than she thought she'd ever be to Francesca again, Sloane thought of nothing but dark curls and constellation freckles. Her stomach flipped as The Gray tugged. Blackness surrounded her for but a moment.

Boiling water sat on the stove of a blue and white patterned kitchen with a terra-cotta tiled floor. Sloane recognized it from the group dinner party photographs Mama Nuccio sent occasionally. Though she knew she couldn't, Sloane took a big deep breath, hoping to smell whatever bubbled next to the pasta water. The strength of memories filled the space where the scents should have been.

Seeing Mama Nuccio's doughy pasta reminded Sloane of the first time she and Francesca tried to make fresh pasta together. Francesca left the room for one minute, and in that incremental period, Sloane overworked the dough.

Unbleached flour coated her hands, and the place looked like her grandmother's kitchen did after rolling out biscuits. Sloane's extra layer of flour overwhelmed the beautiful, fresh eggy smell. Luckily, the aroma of Francesca's sweet basil and robust tomato sauce filled their home soon after.

"No!" Mama Nuccio shouted at Francesca. Sloane had gotten so swept up, she'd almost forgot she wasn't making pasta with Francesca—Mama was. Sloane wasn't even there; she was in the in-between space.

Francesca stopped untangling and counting out silverware. "Exactly. You could have said no."

"No—the silverware. You should know better. Use the set from the china cabinet." Mama Nuccio precariously balanced on a footstool with her arm deep in the top shelf of the cupboard above the refrigerator. "How could I have said no? We asked about dinner in the first place." She pulled back and steadied herself.

"But she invited us over, so we could have suggested to meet out for dinner. Not our fault that some teenager drove into her garage door."

"Never!" Mama Nuccio always had a flair for the dramatic. "That would be horribly rude!"

"How exactly? Never mind. This is what you get, though." And what Francesca got, apparently. Shadows under her eyes made them dull. She could use a nap. Sloane knew that face well, and it usually ended in one angry Italian angel barely making it to the bed.

"Fine, fine. Did you find the silverware?" Mama Nuccio mumbled something about showering and setting the table so quickly Sloane barely understood it all. "Oh!" She threw up her hands. "Decorations!"

"You're kidding!" Francesca slipped into English.

Mama Nuccio replied in Italian, wearing a stern, annoyed expression. "In the closet, down the hall. There are lights, candles, bowls for candies–"

"Is this a wedding?" Francesca's slender fingers rested on her cocked hip. Sloane imagined them on her own and sighed.

She ignored Francesca's snark. "Flowers! Go pick some flowers and put them in those pitchers," she urged, pointing to a pair of hand-painted cream and flower patterned porcelain tea pitchers.

Sloane thought to try and move something again, brush Francesca's hair, move a spoon, but she was rapt with the normalcy of the preparation process. Life moved forward without her. Was it possible she'd already missed her window? Francesca's sad eyes the moment Mama Nuccio turned around to stir the sauces gave Sloane a glimmer of hope.

Through the glass of the French doors, Sloane craned her neck to watch Francesca's shape move under a pink sky. A breeze shifted Francesca's hair into her face. Sloane's fingers itched to push it behind her ears, just how she liked. Francesca tossed her head back, as she'd already gotten dirt on her hands. The long, loose curl slipped right back into the center of her face, splitting her near mirror freckles.

On the side of the house sat Mama Nuccio's modest garden. Though Francesca tended to kill anything alive and green, Mama had taught her how to cut the stems of flowers so they'd live through the butchery.

Francesca was only outside a moment–a place The Gray wouldn't allow Sloane to follow–before she strolled back in with a small array of blue and purple flowers with a few sprigs of a white weed-ish plant.

She sighed as she took in the scent of the exotic-looking flower bunch.

"Got 'em," she mumbled to herself in English. "I'm going to finish up and get ready," she said aloud, back in Italian, to Mama.

Sloane left Francesca to dress the table so she could explore the sprawling home–her new home? Mama Nuccio had done well for herself. Four pale, minimally decorated bedrooms looked similar, with luxurious fabric, one had an en-suite. Even the guest bathroom had a rain shower and a glass bowl sink. Mama had little in the way of overhead lighting, just large windows and skylights, grand lamps scattered in corners, and sweet vanity lamps on hand-carved tables. It reeked of wealth Sloane had no idea she possessed.

Water hit tile in the far bathroom of the house. Sloane followed the beating sound, her heart matching its rhythm. Francesca's clothes were piled by a towel on the floor. Between The Gray and steam, the shower walls were nearly opaque. Sloane put her hand on the glass, imagining Francesca doing the same.

Her breath quickened as she searched for a space where the fog wasn't thick. A tiny smear rewarded her with the naked shape of Francesca. Curves and matted curls would have stopped Sloane's heart right then if she'd been alive. But metal squealed, and the water dripped away. Just a quick shower, it seemed. Francesca stepped out and squeezed her hair. Sloane used to try and beat her to that; she enjoyed playing with Francesca's wet hair.

Non-corporeal hands slid along the space beside Francesca's body. Sloane shivered with memories but shook them off. She'd gone down that road and only frustrated herself.

"Sloane?" Francesca's eyes were wide. Her hands slid down her hips, but she laughed. "Right. Been down that road before," Francesca said to herself as she grabbed the nearest towel and covered the beauty of her skin from Sloane.

Sloane lurked in the corner, watching her lover dress. It had become so normal for both of them that they flirted while they did it. Now, Francesca threw on clothes unceremoniously. Sloane left the room sadder than she'd been before, and finished roaming the house.

After the tour, she charged the closed doors again. No matter how hard she tried, her feet couldn't move over the threshold, as if they'd been bolted to the ground. The garden, Francesca's beautifully decorated dinner table, the oncoming candy sunset were all just out of reach. They were so high up on a nearly mountainous hill, they could see every house, shop, and ruin as if it were a miniature of itself, but Sloane had to see it with an obstructed view.

Ding, dong.

Sloane slid toward the front door to observe the dinner guests. Francesca jogged to the door and tugged at her yellow shift dress. Two wet strands of darkened hair dangled partially out of her bun in the back.

They'd tickle her neck once or twice during the evening. Without Sloane there, Francesca would probably assume a bug found her delicious.

A deep inhale puffed Francesca's chest before she put her hand on the knob; it visibly shook. No wonder she was wearing the teardrop diamond earrings Sloane had given to her for their third anniversary. According to Francesca, happy memories equaled positive vibes.

A chorus of hellos sounded through the entryway before she'd fully opened the door.

"Come, come. What are you drinking? I have a few kinds of

vinos we picked up at a few tours we took today." Laughter followed Mama Nuccio's comment as she ushered her guests in around the stock still Francesca. "Red or white would be a good place to start."

The consensus: red. Francesca took another deep breath and put on her best hostess smile—all teeth and round cheeks. Once, after she and Sloane had hosted a small gathering at a nearby park, Francesca had told her she never wanted to smile again. She'd insisted they watch depressing romantic dramas with a sad twist of death or miscommunication for the rest of the evening.

"Good evening, Francesca. Don't you look breathtaking?" a classically handsome, tall man asked. Dark brown Fabio hair framed his face and hung just below his ears. Sloane didn't like how his eyes twinkled at Francesca. Taken and not straight, thanks.

"Thanks." Francesca slugged him on the shoulder. Sloane snickered loudly; she covered her mouth out of instinct even as The Gray devoured it. "You don't look too bad yourself. I heard through the grapevine there was wine. Ha! Look at me, making bad jokes, and I stopped drinking a few hours ago. Better get some wine in everyone so I'm funny again."

"I'll grab us something," the man said. "Then I can introduce you."

"Nonsense!" said a perfectly aged, tan woman. The resemblance to the man was uncanny.

"Alma, I presume?" Francesca asked, smiling.

The woman wore a bright blue maxi dress that would have dragged the floor if it weren't for her wedged heels. So chic. Her hair rested in loose, soft curls on her shoulders.

She took Francesca's hand. "My dear, it is so nice to meet you. I feel I know you already. I'm so sorry about Susan."

Francesca took a full step backwards, snatched her hand

back, threw it to her chest, and paled to Sloane's color. At the same moment, Sloane's eyes bulged as she gasped into The Gray. Who was that woman? How did she know her real name?

"I overstepped!" Alma admonished herself. "I barely meet you, and I presume... I just feel like I–"

"You called her Susan."

"That's–that was her name, was it not?"

Francesca sputtered out the word yes. "Very few people kn– She went by Sloane. Even I wasn't allowed to call her Susan." She chuckled to hide her obvious hurt.

A wave of stones crushed Sloane's chest. She never wanted Francesca to feel she wasn't allowed to do something. Still, that's what she'd asked, wasn't it?

Alma shook her head, and said, "I'm sorry. It won't happen again."

"No... I mean, thank you," Francesca stumbled as she stared at her bare feet.

Her toenails were painted a coral. Sloane felt a moment of pride that Francesca had remembered to do that for herself. She must have done it during Sloane's frustrating time stuck in San Francisco.

"Could we start over?" Alma asked.

"I'd like that. A lot."

She coughed. "Hi, I'm Alma–a friend of your mother's."

Long past time for Sloane to leave, she retreated to Francesca's room. Francesca could make it through an evening–shakily, but she could. Sloane just knew she had to make contact before Francesca was okay enough to open the door without a taking a pause.

THE BEDROOM DOOR SLAMMED SHUT.

It was the moment Francesca left her all over again. Sloane seemed to be unable to go through walls or doors once they had been closed. Hoping this time would be different, she tried to run through it, but could only bounce into an invisible wall, unable to reach the doorknob she couldn't interact with.

No—not again. It couldn't be so simple. It couldn't be so easy to trap her for hours, days, weeks at a time.

Sloane felt a scream build inside of her. Usually, she'd smother it with a pillow, snuff it out until she could calm herself again. But the unknowing helplessness of The Gray wouldn't allow it; she had to release it aloud. The sounds that ripped through her should have shattered the glass panes of the only window in the room. Instead, the scream became a slight whir around her. Part of Sloane even convinced herself her throat hurt from the strain.

When a curtain shifted, she stopped, unsure if it was her hard efforts or the Tuscan summer wind blowing through the cracked window. As much as she wanted it to be her, it wasn't; after she'd stopped screaming, the sheer fabric had still moved. She needed concrete proof that she had an impact on the living world, as it had on her. Sloane should have stayed with Francesca and her party, watched her enjoy her evening as if Sloane had never been. She felt forgotten and weak.

She crawled on the tall bed, lying on Francesca's usual side of the bed because she now slept on Sloane's. Her hand fell into the impression of Francesca's body, and the ball of grief bounced back in. Nausea she'd become accustomed to feeling most hours settled in her stomach first.

The door to the bedroom flung open. Sloane barely noticed it, as if it were the ghost and not she.

The sound of Francesca's laughter made Sloane turn to see a familiar sight. Francesca held a ring Sloane's grandmother had given her. Sloane watched as the smokey grey stone on a delicate tarnished band hovered over Francesca's ring finger. With a quick frown at herself in the mirror, she slid it onto her right ring finger. Francesca leaned forward and held onto the dresser.

"It's okay; it's okay; it's okay," she said to herself in the mirror. She shook her head. "I love you, Sloane. You know that, don't you?"

A tear slipped down her naked face and dropped to the floor. Standing up straight, she wiped it away and took in a shaky breath. Sloane knew that sound of bravery well; she'd heard it echoing off the walls of abandoned buildings many times as a teen.

Francesca would have a different ring on her ring finger–an engagement ring–if only the truck driver had one more nap or one less beer.

Sloane could remember staring at her body, and then the ring. Francesca had been within reaching distance of it but didn't know to look for it. The small shining symbol of everything Sloane had felt since the moment she'd seen Francesca in the grocery store checkout line had been right beside a piece of broken glass.

It had taken years, but Sloane had finally found what to say, how to propose properly. Just imagining the practiced words had Sloane caught between grief and rage.

As if made of sunlight, her pain began to radiate: legs heavy, arms weak, ribs cracking. The heat of the loss had her eyes burning, as every muscle collapsed in on itself. Both lungs would have become useless chunks of meat if she'd been alive.

If ever there was a time to connect with the world, it was that moment.

Sloane screamed into the abyss as she pushed through The Gray's blur and punched a pillow. A different kind of cry released from her as she created an indention–nothing near the size of her fist, but it was a start.

A voice came from a whisper of a shape. "Are you all right?"

"Of course I'm not okay," Sloane shouted before she realized someone had addressed her.

A lightning fear struck her. She had no place to run, to hide.

"Do not be afraid," a quiet voice called from a flickering shadow–the same one she'd been ignoring for months.

Sloane backed up against the headboard and curled into a ball. Francesca strode out of the room, unaware of the horror going on around her. It happened so quickly, Sloane didn't have time to think and run out. When the door closed again, Sloane felt ill. She'd missed another window. Now no one could help her; she was utterly alone–except for the voice.

"What... uh, who are you?"

Had she gone crazy? Could that happen in The Gray? Had her voice always been deeper than Francesca's? Her throat itched. With her toned, tattooed arms and manly voice, Sloane had the desire to tug at the turquoise dress she wished she wasn't stuck in. Thank God she'd listened to Francesca and not shaved one side of her head. People would constantly have asked her about her sexuality. Whose business was it? Not that she was ashamed in the least–Sloane loved showing Francesca off–but she didn't feel the need to justify her life choices to strangers.

"Does not matter who I am," the shadow replied. It was a feminine voice with a hint of an accent Sloane couldn't place. "It only matters that I can hear you."

The Gray shimmered as the shadow began to form an almost translucent shape of a young girl. Sloane didn't trust the apparition.

"How can you hear me?" Sloane asked.

"I do not know. I have felt ripples of other's grief through the years. Many others." A sigh filled the air. "Their grief threatened to break through the barrier, but none have been able to. You, on the other hand..."

"I don't understand. *My* grief broke a barrier? What barrier? Wouldn't everyone have grief? That's why we're stuck... Right?" She did have unfinished business.

"I do not know. You pierced the wall months ago, but I was unable to make my way through to you." The voice sighed. "I still have not figured out why I cannot leave this side. As a small child, I heard many theories on The Veil in my village before she killed me. It could be any one of them."

"Who killed you?" Sloane asked more demandingly than she'd intended.

The girl faded into almost nothing with a soft heave; the beginning of a sob sounded far away.

"I'm sorry! Please don't go; I don't want to be alone again. She's so close but untouchable. I can't–" Sloane broke away.

"I know," the wisp said. "I watched Papa until he died of loneliness. I thought, surely I could go then, but I stayed on. I have wandered since." Instead of talking more, she calmed her breathing, which had grown erratic.

Sloane wasn't prepared to deal with the thought of Francesca on her deathbed, old, broken, and frail.

They stayed like that: Sloane sitting on the bed and the shadow girl standing in the corner, both crying for their own reasons, until Francesca swooped back into the room to use its bathroom. The door closing behind her shook them from their trances. Being trapped in the room no longer mattered. Sloane would have stayed to talk to the shadow either way. Francesca would be back later. They could sleep beside each other as they always did.

When Francesca rushed back into the party again, the shadow girl asked, "That is her, is it not?"

"Francesca, yeah."

"What happened? What caused the ripple? Something had to."

Shadow Girl was nosy, but Sloane didn't have anyone else.

"Do you mean what happened right before you showed up? Francesca came into the room to get a ring but put it on the wrong finger. But I guess it wasn't wrong; I never had a chance to propose. But then she said she loved me, and it felt so... so..."

"Like she loved another?"

Sloane's arms and legs erupted with goosebumps as she stuttered. "No! What makes you think that? How could she? She doesn't know anyone out there. But it wasn't just that. For some reason, that made me remember something. It was as if I was there again: the night of the crash. I remembered that the ring I had planned to ask her to marry me with was only a few feet away from her. She didn't see it. If she had, she would have known. She'd be wearing it now, not enjoying a dinner party," Sloane lamented, knowing that may not be true. "I just wish I was out there, by her side. She's always been the more social of us. With so many people around, and Mama Nuccio pushing her, she'll move on."

A soothing noise came from the dark shape.

"I just want to touch her again," Sloane said as she stared at the shadow.

The silence needed filling.

"So, what can you tell me about my heartbeat?"

9

FRANCESCA

She stopped by the kitchen for a shot of tequila. The nearby chef's knife stabbed her in the chest at the thought of Sloane. She still couldn't believe herself.

Francesca had no reason not to wear Sloane's ring on her left ring finger, but it was too late to change it. Anyone, or everyone, could have seen the ring by now. The twinkle lights danced and pinged off of every jewel; Alma's necklace glittered, Mama's bracelet became a row of stars, Francesca could only imagine her earrings. So, the ring probably sparkled enough to be noticed too.

She sighed and took another shot, then one more. Sloane would have disapproved, would have said she'd be sloppy soon if she didn't slow down; Sloane wouldn't have been wrong.

Francesca walked slowly so as not to wobble; treating it as a game, she repeated a guests name in her head with each successful step. It would only showcase her drunken state if she forgot them. They'd only just introduced themselves as they stuffed their faces with Mama's fresh ciabatta bread.

The smell of freshly picked olives had filled the house alongside Mama Nuccio's famous sauce which had been simmering on the stove beside the pisella alla florentina since minutes after they'd come back from their wine tours. It had been mouth-watering before the third tequila shot. Her stomach rolled as she steadied herself on the counter's edge. Damn, she'd only made it a few feet.

Sliding to the floor, she listened to the expectant boiling, bubbling water and took a deep breath. Francesca couldn't escape the food, though. A chicken marsala roasted in the oven, even closer now that she'd become a pile of goo on the floor. Her stomach demanded to be emptied. She obliged as soon as she made it to the nearest bathroom—Mama's.

She purged herself of liquor, wine, and none of her guilt. A little pale and sweaty, she splashed water on her face and patted it dry. With the hopes she'd done enough to lessen her sick appearance, Francesca made her way out to the party again—still drunk and nauseous. A dimming pink-orange sky and twinkle lights should allow some leeway.

Marta commented that she'd been right about the dress the moment Francesca stepped foot on the patio again; she assumed her efforts weren't in vain.

Marta spent the next two minutes telling the table what Francesca had purchased at her shop, then gushed about what Mama came back to buy while Francesca was looking in a cute toy shop. When Alma caught Francesca's eye, she rolled hers and winked. Francesca held her breath when she came to the end of the shopping trip, but Marta didn't tell them what she'd spent.

Thank God.

Mama insisted on avoiding the clearance and sale racks.

The bakery owner, Lia, came bearing so many Zeppoles Francesca had a hard time not eating a few before dinner; they wouldn't have been missed.

That was, of course, before the tequila.

Francesca looked longingly at the three white boxes for only a moment before her stomach knotted again. The time for dough and sugar had passed.

Lia brought her boyfriend, Alonzo. He wasn't talkative, but they did squeeze out that he worked at the fish market. In what capacity, who knew.

Alonzo brought a sweet, single guy who lived a few streets down–as if Mama wasn't feeding enough people already. He rarely contributed to the conversation–the man whose name Francesca forgot the moment he said it–but he never stopped smiling.

What felt like, but definitely wasn't, the entire Loreti family sat at the table. The matriarch, Alma; her son, Tony; daughter, Cecelia; nephew, Roberto; and another nephew whose name Francesca missed during a particularly loud chew were a boisterous bunch. They laughed and told stories about their crazy Italian mothers, while those crazy Italian mothers corrected them. Francesca couldn't entirely keep up. She should have listened to Sloane's voice in her head. Sloppy, she verged on being sloppy. No one seemed to notice, or at least they didn't comment.

Marta, Lia, and Alonzo were talking shop, while the Loreti nephews and Cecelia listened on. The nephews told the table about their dreams of one day opening a restaurant like Tony. Mama Loreti said they better get their act together if they were going to do much but beg in the street. "Or I'm cutting you off at 17; I'll get your Mama to do the same!" To which they complained, "But Tony and Cecelia weren't cut off until they were good and ready."

Tony flirted through the pasta Francesca couldn't eat, so she told him about her Barbie's marrying each other. The story had the entire party listening in and roaring with the 'punchline': "I was progressive for my age!"

She'd sobered up enough to carry on a conversation. It had taken an hour, but she contributed. Mama beamed with pride; so her drunken state had not gone unnoticed. Damn.

When the laughter died down, and people went back to their conversations, Tony looked at Francesca.

He scratched at his still too-long mustache and rubbed his beard. "Have you met my sister, Cecelia?"

"Why yes Tony, everyone met everyone at the beginning of the party." Francesca laughed.

"You two should talk."

Francesca stared at him, and his eyes twinkled. "Um, alright. But you and I are talking now. Unless you're bored with me."

"No, no! Anything but! I think you're the star of the party!"

Francesca almost fell out of her seat. Drunk and sick, but the life of the party. Sloane did say that was usually her style.

"Cecelia," Tony said across the table. "This is Francesca."

Large round curls turned away from the conversation Cecelia was having with one of her cousins and bobbed in their direction. Pouty lips turned up into a coy smile.

"Yes, Tone? I wasn't doing anything, what can I help you with?" Such a sibling response.

Francesca chuckled, and Cecelia's soft brown eyes lit up. God help her, Francesca's heart fluttered. She'd already met this woman, but it was different with the lights and the drink, the smirk and the snark.

Instantly horrified by herself, Francesca needed to leave, needed to be anywhere but there.

"I'm so sorry," Francesca said loud enough for all of the guests to hear. "I think the wine has caught up with me. Or maybe I'm just overwhelmed by all of the good conversation."

That earned her a chuckle from the entire group sans Cecelia, whose eyes shifted down immediately.

"I'm getting a bit of a headache, and think I should go retire...
with a few Zeppoles, of course," Francesca added.

A hearty group laugh filled Mama's backyard, followed by
different versions of, "It was so lovely to meet you," "I hope you
feel better," and "Let's have lunch soon."

"It was wonderful to meet you all too. Until our next meeting." Francesca smiled and waved before she grabbed an entire
box of Zeppoles and winked at the table.

More laughter followed her to the kitchen, where she
poured herself a big glass of water. Usually, the group would
have said goodbye for twenty minutes, maybe even an hour, but
Francesca must have looked stricken; she felt it. She left so
abruptly she wondered what Mama would say in the morning.
Hopefully, nothing–a pipe dream.

Ragged tears broke open her ribs before she made it to her
room. She held her Zeppole box like a baby as she slammed the
door shut and curled up on Sloane's side of the bed.

Francesca recalled a moment like that one with giggles
instead of sobs. Sloane had bought her a box of treats from one
of her favorite bakeries–she had four. Sloane had slid into bed as
she'd told a story about the horrible customers in line that had
them all but suffocating with laughter. They'd fed each other the
sweets, getting chocolate shavings and pastry cream everywhere.
When they'd gotten to the powdered sugared doughnuts, Sloane
had played piano on Francesca's coated fingers. White had
dusted their pillows, which had made biting into them all the
more satisfying.

Francesca tasted her salty tears as she stuffed the fried
dough into her face, sickening herself in more ways than one as
she did so. She regretted it as soon as the overly sweet taste hit
her tongue. Powdered sugar thickened to a paste that stuck to
the roof of her mouth. Guilt clung to the rest of her.

"Mm surry," she mumbled into her dampening pillow.

SUNLIGHT POURED in like a laser show, flickering in her vision violently. The base of her skull felt tight and swollen.

The night came back in pieces: Sloane's ring, sparkling conversation, tequila, Cecelia's smile. Pasta and booze churned in Francesca's stomach. She barely made it to the bathroom in time. Mama came to hold her hair before she made it to her second heave.

"Easy does it," Mama cooed. "Let it all out; then we can get you something to ease the cramps."

Francesca worshipped the porcelain god for so long, only acid remained. It just proved that her insides were rotten. Fitting, as she'd betrayed Sloane.

Mama left Francesca half-sobbing to grab her "something". It turned out Mama meant the hair of the dog. She poured a large glass of red wine in a plastic cup and handed it to a still queasy Francesca.

"No Mama, no." She hadn't stopped begging for death yet, and her stomach was still making inhuman noises. "I can barely look at it."

"You'll get used to it–even with the shots you took." Mama winked. "You think Mama would lead you astray? Just drink up. Alma wants to have breakfast, so you need to look better than you do."

"Gee, thanks, Mama," she said in English. "I can't eat right now. Maybe lunch, okay? I just want to go back to sleep. Is there a dark room in this house? I can't take any more sun."

Mama laughed. As she shook her head, loose curls tussled in front of her face. "The wine cellar."

"So helpful today," Francesca called over her shoulder.

After she brushed her teeth three times, Francesca took the wine and a Zeppole from the counter with her back to the bed.

"I knew you'd choose my way! Drink up, and be ready in an hour," Mama chuckled as she shut the door behind her quietly.

Francesca used all of her willpower not to snark again, but yelling might have split her in half. Fine, she'd just crawl under the mass of sheets and pillows. The fluff had suited her grief, so they should be good enough for a migraine.

10
———

SLOANE

Francesca deserved to be curled up, moaning from pain. Though Sloane hated herself for allowing such a thought to creep in, she tried to let herself off the hook. At that moment, she didn't know Francesca at all.

Sloane didn't hide her tears in The Gray, not even from the shadow girl. Still, now they could hear each other. The girl's form hunched on the chair that doubled as a second side table by the bed. Half of her whirred as if she were swinging her legs, and she hummed an eerie lullaby silently to herself.

"It will be all right. Soon enough Francesca will see you once again," the girl promised.

"Who are you?"

"My name is–" She took a long pause. "Molly. I am no one, just another lost soul. I roam untethered."

"How?"

Molly's form shimmered in what Sloane assumed was a shrug.

"I'm Sloane," she said as if Molly had asked. "How long have you been dead?" Instantly, Sloane slapped her hand over her mouth, breathless.

That was crass, too blunt, and the barrier between Sloane and the living made words her heavy as though she'd just run a marathon.

"A long time. Since my name was Erzsébet."

Speechless, Sloane nodded. What could she say next? 'Oh, cool?'

Molly fell quiet again; only broken breaths cut through The Gray. Sloane couldn't tell whose they were. Did Molly still cry after all these years? Would Sloane, if she stayed?

"Papa thought I was part of his fever," she answered an unasked question. "It calmed him to see me, helped ease him to his next place. I thought it would send me to another place too, but I stayed on."

Sloane's imagination exploded with Francesca withered, with a reunion as she lays dying. Her tears were the loudest then, of that, Sloane had no doubt.

The Gray moved with Molly, as her darkness skipped towards Sloane. Her shape became more solid and ghostly rather than the haze of a smoky bar. Sloane finally got a feel for Molly's age, and it was sobering. No older than thirteen, she still had baby cheeks. An ill-fitting corset peasant dress with a full skirt hung off of her undeveloped body. Sloane wished she made herself visible, as she wanted to see more details. As if she were drowning, Sloane clung to the mystery of Molly, her appearance, age, accent, story.

"Shall we leave this place of grief?" Molly asked.

"What?" Sloane had only just stopped crying. "What are you talking about?"

"Let us leave this place. No good comes of you wallowing by your love, who may or may not have betrayed you." Sloane winced. But Molly pressed on. "We will start small, of course. Let us go to the garden. There are some lovely flowers in bloom, and you could pick one."

Molly was insane.

"How is that small?" Sloane changed her mind: she wanted to be alone forever. Maybe she enjoyed wallowing; she wanted to be with Francesca no matter what happened. If her pain made a hole in The Gray, she had to be able to touch her again, eventually.

Francesca's sounds became soft, sweet. They reminded Sloane of the few mornings when she'd wake up earlier than Francesca and watch her sleep. She'd twitch from vivid dreams, but her breath would remain steady and quiet. Often, Francesca had polka dot silver dollar sized drool stains on both sides of her pillow and woke with slime on her face.

Francesca sat up and stretched. "Okay! I'm up. A quick shower and I'm ready."

She stuffed a Zeppole in her face and took a long swig of wine as she padded towards the shower.

Sloane watched Francesca move. A mess of curls was knotted on the right side of her head. She grabbed a brush, dress, and pair of underwear. They were her period panties, which pleased Sloane.

Molly reached out and spun the paper-thin lampshade on the floor lamp that stood behind the bathroom door. But as Francesca had already flicked on the vanity lights and turned on her electric toothbrush, she missed the display.

"It is small because you have already traveled a long way. Picking a flower should be a simple task compared to that," Molly said. Her vague, unknown accent had faded behind the smile in her voice.

Sloane's eyes flicked from Francesca to the wobbling lampshade. Her heart caught in her throat. To keep her burning eyes from spilling desires, she asked Molly where she was from. It was abrupt enough Molly seemed nearly taken off guard. "Your speech patterns and accent don't match up."

"I watch television. I enjoy modern shows now and again."

Sloane almost laughed. It hadn't occurred to Sloane that she could watch along with Francesca. Though Francesca hadn't watched anything on their old laptop-turned-tv since the accident, so it wouldn't have mattered.

"Now, shall we? You are getting no closer to Francesca just sitting here."

"Fine. But I don't know how I got here, so it's not as if I can just do that again." Sloane felt hopeless; she should give in to her non-existence. The pain that hovered right below the skin only needed a light scratch, and the bleeding may never stop.

"I CAN'T," Sloane shouted through Francesca's bedroom door.

Molly waited on the other side. As if a stern parent somewhat holding her anger back, she said, "Try harder. Think of your Francesca." She probably had her small hand on her curveless hip.

Sloane focused and remembered it as though it were only moments before, and she hated Molly for having her tap into it. But it was her choice which memory she picked, wasn't it? Molly had only told her to immerse herself, and Sloane chose the worst moment of her life. A trivial fight that had escalated to words she couldn't take back: "Leave then! Go be with that girl!"

Watching Francesca's shoulders slump had crushed Sloane. They'd agreed not to talk about the girl again; they'd promised. The whole subject had still been so raw. She remembered thinking, "This is it; we're over. I've lost her for good. I've messed up a lot–we both have–but this is the last straw. How can I apologize for that?"

Closing her eyes, Sloane stepped towards the wooden door and felt no resistance. When she unscrunched her face, Molly stood in front of her. More opaque than she'd been thus far, her crooked teeth beamed at Sloane.

Still thinking about nearly ruining their relationship, about making love to Francesca, Sloane ripped through The Gray faster than she believed she could. Her body felt raw, bloody, by the time she reached the glass sliding doors. They were still wide open; Mama Nuccio ever the trusting woman.

"After you," Molly said.

Sloane stepped over the threshold of the back doors. If The Gray was absent, floral perfume and the moist scent of the earth would fill her senses; still, she took a deep, fruitless breath.

The watercolor-painted backyard with dirty brush splashes, the purples and blues, pinks and oranges wasn't as vivid as it should have been. Still, the lush garden had small patches of green that prevailed through The Gray, as if too defiant to be dulled.

A beautiful statue of a nude faerie lounged in the center. Sloane leaned down to see the carved butterflies on the faerie's shoulders and ivy draped around her breasts. As if the stone girl had been there forever, lichen had already begun to climb up chubby legs, reaching for her right hand which hung lazily by her side.

Mama Nuccio had always had a green thumb. When she visited Francesca, she'd bring their sad, brown houseplants to life. They'd bloom as if by magic, reaching towards the sky and bursting with flowers and bright leaves.

The moment she left, they would die–from rebellion or Sloane and Francesca's black thumbs, they never could tell. Either way, unless Mama came to visit, they avoided plants that hadn't been cut and prepped by a store.

Sloane's mood shifted.

Years back, Francesca found a small, out of the way garden. French pink snapdragons grew in hidden corners, while poppies large enough to put Dorothy to sleep and bushes filled the open spaces. A spongy moss-covered angel statue was tucked under a weathered stone bench half-sunken in the dirt. Smashed together, they stayed there until sunset.

They were only able to visit it a few times before the city paved over it, which meant they'd guessed right: the owner had passed away, leaving the well-loved garden behind. When they'd driven by and saw the parking lot, Sloane realized they hadn't taken pictures of anything but the angel–she'd never been so sentimental.

Molly cleared her throat at Sloane's slip into the past. "Perhaps you would like to try and pick one? The pink one, maybe?"

"I'd rather see Francesca." Her hands slid behind her back as if she stood in a house of glass, and she shuffled her feet.

Without letting Molly get another word in, Sloane began to focus. If memories were her new form of strength, she had six years worth to choose from.

Apartment shopping had been easy, despite living in San Francisco. Sloane had closed her eyes in each space, and she'd known if she'd feel safe or not. A small square of a room fit her best.

Francesca had moved Sloane's things in after her own. She knew Sloane had abandonment issues so deep no therapy session seemed to help. The fear that she'd get settled just in time for Francesca to announce she'd had enough of her loomed around her like the shroud of The Gray.

When Sloane had still been Susan, her mother had decided age fifteen was old enough to take care of herself. The school hadn't known, and Sloane hadn't been about to tell them. She'd finished her last two years of school at her family home, until the rent checks her mother had been sending had stopped coming. Her next few years were spent bouncing from friend's couches to tear-downs insufficient to keep her safe.

Never once had Sloane cried to anyone about her problems–not because she'd been strong, but because no one would have cared.

After high school, she'd gotten a job and stayed at a friend's house until she could make rent money. She'd already begun the painstaking process of meeting new people and reinventing herself as Sloane No-Last-Name. So by the time she'd become happily independent by choice, she had become who she wanted to be. Even so, she'd shielded herself from closeness.

When she'd let Francesca in, she still had a weak fence around her. But the day her last box of clothes sat in the middle of the half-finished apartment–three years after the fumbling grocery store conversation–any barriers had crumbled, and she'd become completely Francesca's. Moreover, Sloane had finally told Francesca the pathetic story of her real name.

"Congratulations seem to be in order." Molly made a noise of approval and nodded.

A tear as thin as her eyebrows were blonde slid down Sloane's nose; she'd managed to leave the house.

Francesca and Mama Nuccio were meandering down a beautiful lane with gelato. Francesca had ordered bacio, no doubt, and Mama had vanilla or vanilla–an adventurous woman with dessert, that one.

Aside from Francesca, Sloane missed food the most–more than the scent of a garden or a clear view of the sunset. In Italy, there seemed to be no escape from mouthwatering dishes.

She refrained from stomping her feet as she wouldn't get the craved satisfying sound.

A yellow-brown stucco covered nearly all of the buildings surrounding them. Picture boxes hung from most windows; multi-colored flowers struggled to break through the fog of The Gray. Every movie about Italy had to have been filmed on that street–though her location remained to be seen.

Swept up in the sights and sounds, Sloane became a newborn thrust into a cold, harsh world, snatched from where she wanted to be.

Sloane attempted a smile. "So, do you go all over?"

Though Molly looked too young to have memories strong enough, she had no issues navigating The Gray.

"Why have you brought us here?"

No questions then; that was fine with Sloane. She shuffled behind a laughing Francesca. Missing the sound of her footsteps on the slate ground, she sighed. "I wanted to be near her. I always do, though."

"Why not interact with her? Try her hair or the straps of her bag." Molly shielded half of her mouth as though she were telling a secret.

Desire saddened Sloane. So many failed attempts discouraged more.

Mama Nuccio and Francesca stopped at an imported Venetian mask kiosk. Sloane sidled between them. Inches away from her love, a dark cloud with the smallest ray of sun hung above her.

Francesca's freshly shampooed hair smelled like nothing. Lazy curls were beginning to frizz in the unfamiliar heat; Sloane reached to smooth them—even though Francesca would inevitably whine about her doing so. Sloane's attempts made no impact. She watched the small muscles of Francesca's back as she picked up a white porcelain mask. Hand-painted swirls were mixed in with music notes and dotted with pearlescent beads. For maximum tourist appeal, they'd added glitter. Long curled ribbons hung from the bottom.

"How much?" Francesca asked, and Sloane almost melted.

They'd had that exact moment so many times. Francesca would look at a beautiful trinket during their vacation and ask, "How much?".

It never mattered. Sloane may try to haggle, depending on their location, but Francesca never left without her souvenir.

A confused accent broke the spell. "What is wrong?"

"I was just–" Sloane didn't know how to describe getting lost to a young girl. "I was just admiring her."

Molly's nose wrinkled as though she'd smelled something sour. "All right."

Piano ready fingers reached into an unfamiliar purse to pull out an elephant patterned turquoise wallet Sloane bought her in New York. Francesca made a sharp inhale as she held it.

Mama Nuccio popped her wrist with The Letter. "I gave you money for when you are alone, Essie, not with me. I pay when we are together."

Sloane remembered that letter and the stories of Francesca trying to sneak a peek at it. Mama Nuccio had told Sloane what the letter said six months before the accident. They were in her lavish San Francisco hotel room where Francesca snored lightly on the queen bed next to Mama's.

"I can drink this much wine and more usually. I don't understand!" Mama had had one too many martinis. "Sloane," she'd said. "I've held a secret for a long time. But I'm going to tell you. I just need you to promise you'll let me tell Francesca when I'm ready."

Sloane had kept that promise. Watching Francesca's chocolate eyes cut towards the letter made Sloane think Mama Nuccio hadn't been ready yet.

"Well?" Molly complained again.

Sloane was grateful she couldn't hear her heeled boots tapping.

As if photos, Sloane began flipping through memories. Before Sloane could find one, before she could try touching her hair again, Francesca turned around. She stood less than a shared breath away, but The Gray kept them separate.

In life, Francesca would have said, 'Your lips can't be that close to me and not kiss me; that's not fair, is it?'

Francesca's brow wrinkled, the way it did when her premature arthritic knee sensed rain. Her mouth pursed as she swiveled, and her face slid right through Sloane's. Though Sloane stepped back clutching her chest, Francesca just shook her body and wiggled her arms.

"Mama?"

Sloane stood caught in the cross-hairs, and Mama Nuccio made a noise of questioning.

Closing her eyes, Francesca puffed up. "Thank you for the mask."

11

FRANCESCA

Francesca continued, "–Because it was her turn! We all died laughing. I said, 'Sloane, that doesn't matter. You can't just–'"

"Not that I don't find the tale of Sloane's gameplay fascinating, but that's the third story you've told about her without taking a breath. What's going on, Essie?" Muma asked with a serious tone.

Francesca almost snarked, 'What do you think?' Instead, she cut herself off; the unfinished story left her stuck.

"Essie, talk to me."

Francesca took a step forward to hide her watering eyes. Dead ruins like broken tombstones stuck out from dried grass. Sorrow tinged the air around them. Grand buildings had once lived there. But, as with everything good in life, they'd crumbled–their destruction quick.

Lights flashed, a horn, shattering–"Sloane loves ruins, loves anything old." Francesca tuned her anti-lullaby out and slipped into a world where Sloane was at home waiting for her. "I mean our apartment should tell you that. It smells like an antique store. I always wanted to tell her that my eyes watered when I dusted the bookshelves, but I couldn't have handled the look on her face. Besides, the amount of money we spent on old books, I tell you, Mama. If she'd even thought to get rid of them for me... God, I can't imagine. My wallet might weep." Francesca forced a chuckle.

Mama sighed in response. She sat on the ground, leaned against a gate to nothing, and patted the less rocky side of her.

Francesca slid down to the only mildly uncomfortable space. Sickness welled up in her gut, warning her that tears were on their way. She didn't know what to say. How could Francesca tell Mama she sensed Sloane while she picked out her mask, or that she felt guilty for looking at Cecelia? She had to deal silently and in her own way.

"I can't wait to go home and tell Sloane–" Her hand flew up to her mouth. She'd just been thinking about her life without Sloane; what the hell was that? "But she isn't... she won't be... she's... Mama, Sloane's dead." Francesca avoided the word, so her face ached as it burst through a clenched jaw.

"I know, Essie, I know. The hurt will lessen."

"When?" Francesca laid her head on Mama's bosom as hot, angry-at-God tears slid from her resistant eyes.

Mama stroked her hair. "Only time can tell. But you will have these moments long past then too." She spoke with an experienced voice. "You've already begun to heal, I've seen it. The party showed me how far you've come. You have a long climb ahead of you yet, but you're doing so well, Es."

"Am I? I feel like eleven months have disappeared from my life, and I can barely remember them. I don't think I should want to, though. Which way helps the healing more?" Francesca asked. She peeled herself from her mother's tear-crusted shirt and heaved herself up by the wrought iron bars of the homeless gate.

Mama reached her hands up for a pull.

The child-like act made Francesca smile. After the tug, she brushed the dust from the ground off of her light blue skirt and began walking away. "You coming?"

Despite her long legs, Francesca took four skips to catch up. "Where are we going in such a hurry?"

"To have lunch, of course. The gelato didn't stick like I'd hoped." Mama looked down at her shirt. "And to buy a new top; this one's sad."

They'd had lunch only three hours before the gelato. Whatever they ate would be more of a snack, if Francesca was hungry. She was not. Besides, her jeans were already fitting tightly, and she'd only been in Italy a few days.

A week ago, she would have denied the possibility of too much pasta or Zeppoles or gelato.

Maybe Sloane was right, she was wrong sometimes.

AT LEAST THEY DROVE.

Mama announced they should have lunch less than an hour after they'd eaten full meals. They'd walked and shopped, she'd reasoned. Another half hour of strolling and Francesca matched her mother's perfect Italian image.

"Okay, I could go for a snack."

"Finally; I'm starving!" Mama said. "Let's go find somewhere good."

She'd driven straight to a busy tourist-filled plaza about thirty minutes from her villa. So, when she asked, "How's here?" of course it was, "Great".

"I'm going to find a parking space, freshen my makeup, and oh, I have to grab something from the store there–" She pointed to a row of little shops across the way. "So you go on in and get us a table. They've Americanized their system a bit, so it shouldn't be hard to figure out."

"I wouldn't mind going with you. Or we could do it after; you just said you were starving."

"Yes, but I want to have a nice dinner tonight, so I'm going to make sure we have what we need." Leave it to Mama to already be planning dinner at second-lunch.

Francesca nodded and headed towards the unassuming square building. She and Sloane would have called it 'shambly' because there were several places right outside of San Fran that had the same feel. It needed safer stairs, unbroken windows, a paint job, un-cracked walls, and a roof that wouldn't blow away with a strong wind. But it had charm in a don't-look-too-hard kind of way.

The sign right inside of the door told her to seat herself and order at the counter. She dropped her purse off at a ripped, half-flattened booth close to the counter to hold the table. The kid behind the register devoured her with his eyes as though she were his last meal. He gave her a wink and something free after she ordered a lasagne. Though he probably thought that was a big deal, Francesca wasn't listening. She'd tuned in to a vaguely familiar voice behind her.

"Hey!"

Francesca didn't turn, though. Who did she know in Italy? Mama, that's who. But when the voice said her name, she put it together and tried not to run away.

Over her shoulder, Francesca said, "Cecelia, hi."

"How are you doing? Crazy seeing you here! I come here all the time on my lunch break."

Mama! How could do this she right after she'd cried about Sloane? Oh, she'd hear it. She'd hear all about it. Keeping her rage in check, because it certainly wasn't Cecelia's fault her mother dropped her in an awkward situation, Francesca nodded.

"So, how are you?" Cecelia probed again.

She searched for positivity. "I'm okay." Wasn't terrible. "You said work? What do you do?" And that should do it for her social obligations. She would listen, nod, and make eye contact twice. Once she grabbed her food, Cecelia would leave.

"I work on my family's vineyard. Depending on the day, I do anything from bookkeeping to grape stomping."

That explained the pulled back messy bun, no makeup, vaguely frumpy loose jeans, and tank top. All of which should have made her less attractive–should have.

"Cool."

"Order number 52," the teenage boy with acne called loudly. High school probably sucked for him.

"That's me. It was good seeing you."

"Wait, Francesca?"

Cecelia had a look in her eyes Francesca had seen so many times before. To her horror, a scenario involving lips popped into her head.

"Yeah?" Francesca acted about as casual as a kid in puberty.

"Order 52!" It seemed the kid was angry she didn't return his affections. Or maybe he just wanted her food off the counter. "Sorry, I've got to grab it before he tosses it in the trash."

"Of course, I can wait."

Damn it.

Francesca stepped from the silverware station and grabbed the red plastic tray. Melted cheese seemed to have expanded from her large plate to the tray itself. There was so much of it. She wanted to pick it up and shove it in her face; forks be damned! But Cecelia shuffled her feet steps away, waiting.

"So... I was wondering if, maybe you might want to go with me–"

The lasagne smelled so good' Francesca concentrated on that.

Quickly, Cecelia added, "I mean, if you aren't busy soon, would you like to go out with me sometime? Soon, I mean. Uh, maybe tomorrow, even? Or next week?" she added when Francesca blinked at her plate of meat and cheese.

The restaurant became a supermarket, and Cecelia became Sloane. Francesca may have even smiled at the memory. But the plastic freezer burn scented cardboard brightly lit store was a shack of a restaurant that smelled like tomato and parmesan. "No. I mean–I'm just not ready to date." Francesca would not cry. She would not cry. Okay, she may cry a little.

"I didn't mean to upset you!" Cecelia rushed her way.

"Order 57."

Cecelia's head tilted ever so slightly to see her number; she looked pained.

Impatient, the pimply teen waited less time than before. "Order 57!" He didn't need to be so antsy. There weren't but six people in the entire restaurant.

"You go get that. I'm going to sit. It was nice seeing you."

Francesca almost apologized for tearing up, but she and Sloane had made a pact they would work on only apologizing when they should. Both had the tendency to say sorry to couches if they bumped into them. It had been a problem.

With a tray of salad and a small bowl of pasta salad, Cecelia saddled up to the booth before Francesca had her first bite. Steam had already gone, and the food grew colder with every awkward second.

"I'm sorry, I didn't mean to make you cry. Whatever it was, a bad breakup, recent, whatever, I'm sorry."

"She died," Francesca whispered. The second time she used that word in one day.

Faster than most would have thought to speak, Cecelia said, "I had no idea."

"If Mama hadn't told you, how could you?"

"Do you want to talk about it? Oh God, people ask you that all the time. How about this, do you want me to go? Well, that's not a fair question either. Is it okay if I eat here? Is Mama Nuccio coming? No, that's not fair either; I should just go."

"She should be here soon," Francesca hoped aloud. "And sure, you can eat here. But I'm not up for talking, sor-" She caught herself; she wasn't sorry. If she didn't want to gush to therapists, why would she to the pretty girl across the table? Cecelia only made Francesca's world confusing.

Cecelia took the food off of the tray and started shoveling the overdressed salad in as if her life depended on it. Through a mouth of greens, she mumbled, "Sorry, haven't eaten all day."

And here Francesca had already had pancakes, bacon, and eggs, almost an entire loaf of freshly baked bread slathered in scratch-made butter, spaghetti with meat sauce, Bacio gelato, and had moved on to lasagne. Poor Cecelia.

Mama still hadn't joined them by the time they had finished their food in silence.

"Thank you for letting me sit with you. No pressure, but I'm craving these little pastries a baker down the street makes. I had planned to eat them by the well over there–it's considered a landmark of Montepulciano–because it's such a lovely day. If you want to join me, you can. We don't have to talk, just get the sweets."

She nearly said no.

Francesca had zero room for anything; her stomach already turned thanks to her second lunch. Mama had abandoned her, though, and Cecelia seemed to have mastered the art of not talking.

"Sure, thanks." She'd sounded more enthused about a pap smear before. Oh well.

They strolled a fair distance apart. Sun rays beat down on Francesca's burned, exposed shoulders. The heat and over-stuffing made her drowsy, and thoughts of Sloane had her on the verge of tears. A sad afternoon nap seemed in order. She'd been up too long, done too much already.

"It's just up here," Cecelia said. "If you aren't hungry, you don't have to go in. I won't be but a minute."

"Thanks. I'd love something doughy."

"I'll get you something wrapped up," Cecelia said laughing. The squeals of unruly children nearby dared to swallow it. "Want to find us a table near the well? Maybe a space on the steps? Looks kind of busy today."

Loads of Americans looking for an escape crowded around the well. Camera flashes–unnecessary in the high sun–washed out the majestic lion statues sitting atop the structure. Francesca shifted her weight from one leg to the other on the multicolored cracked stone, mostly obscured by tourists, as she waited for an opening to squeeze her way to the front to peer inside. She imagined a deep and bellowing sound would echo back if she yelled down it.

Stubby, low steps spanned the length of the building across from the well. So many people huddled around the landmark, few found a reason to sit. One round child sat with a dripping waffle cone in his hand, while a woman beside him snapped photos of herself with an old digital camera. After clicking buttons for a moment, she stopped and smiled. Her smug look disappeared the moment put away her camera and looked up to the hustle and bustle.

Francesca nabbed a space a few feet away from Sticky Fingers and Narcissist. Between her bloated stomach and purse, she hoped she saved enough room; Cecelia was small.

"Over here! Cecelia!" she called when she could see the leggy Italian. She carried a large bag with a brown stamped logo on it.

Cecelia waded her way to Francesca attempting to hold eye contact the entire time; Francesca decided to turn her attention to a couple canoodling against a pillar. A moment with Sloane against bricks under a bright streetlamp slid to the forefront of her mind.

Cecelia broke Francesca's thoughts in two. "What a crowd today! I thought it looked busy, but not crazy."

"Never looks as bad from the side streets." Francesca surveyed a man tugging at his khaki shorts. "It's so much quieter on those."

Cecelia nodded and opened the bag. "You want your sweet now or later?"

Was there supposed to be a later? "Now," Francesca said.

"I got you Struffoli." Cecelia grabbed a napkin and handed her both. "I hope you enjoy them. Sticky, but worth it. The baker is from Naples."

A small breeze blew the napkin up. They both reached for it, but Francesca dropped her hand quickly. "I'm sure it's delicious, thank you." She tried not to grimace; more food would make her stomach do rollercoaster drop somersaults.

Lapsing back into silence, they ate their desserts slowly. The tiny balls of crispy dough were officially in the rotation of sweets Francesca would order after only three bites. She tried not to moan. Sloane would have known the face with or without the sound. They were in sync in that, and so many other ways.

As they ate, in as much silence as was possible with crunchy desserts, Cecelia pointed people out and commented on their outfit or their shopping bags. She had a thing for shoes and knew every store in town. Francesca wasn't sure if she would have bragged about that. To each their own. She was reaching, looking for a trait to dislike Cecelia for, but coming back with wisps of smoke.

"So, we've sat here for quite a while... Mama Nuccio has clearly abandoned you. I'm sorry." Cecelia tried to hide her smirk.

Francesca shrugged. "I can get home. I know she's planning a big dinner, so maybe it's best I stay away for a while. If I eat another bite, I may pop, as Sloane would say." Her hand flew up to cover her mouth. Again. She couldn't stop herself lately.

"You can talk about her, you know." Great, another therapist moment. "Or not." Cecelia raised a hand. "I understand not wanting to talk. I went to therapy for a while after my friend died when I was a teenager. That's how they started every session. It was so annoying! All I wanted to do was *not* talk about it."

Francesca laughed, and it felt good. "They do that, don't they? I'm going through therapists like gallons of milk. I use them for one glass and then wonder why I bought them at all." She made a disgruntled sound. "That wasn't a great analogy."

"I got it, though." Cecelia shrugged and smiled.

"I'm glad. Mostly, I want to talk about Sloane in my own time. I want to talk about her all the time and never again. But I don't want someone to tell me it's okay. Of course, it's okay. Freedom of speech or whatever," Francesca rambled. "I just want to tell the important stories, not the big stories. You know?"

A group of high school kids ran past them. One shouted that she loved Tyler. He turned and raised her hand shouting he loved Susan back. Her heart sank.

Who named their kid Susan anymore? It just seemed like a cosmic joke. Fuck the cosmos.

"Are you all right?" Cecelia asked.

Tears were streaming down Francesca's face, so she couldn't

do anything but shake her head. When Cecelia reached out, Francesca pulled back.

"Sloane's name was Susan. She hated it. It took me years of trying to drag it out of her to find out why she hated it so much. Finally, after ages, she told me it was because her drug-addled mother threw out that name to the nurse with no thought at all. She'd watched a Manson documentary the night before and could pretty much only think of the name Susan Atkins. It sounds like it would be a funny anecdote at parties, but no, it couldn't be, because her mother left her." For the first time since Cecelia had given Francesca the Struffoli, Francesca turned to look at her. "I'm the only person who ever truly loved her. And I'm not sure I was enough."

Cecelia did the unthinkable. She pulled Francesca into a hug and let her cry about her dead love.

When she tired of crying in public, Francesca sat up straight. Tears and snot dripped onto her dress. She didn't bother wiping them away. Smiling through the ache, she said, "Sloane would be laughing at me right now."

"Oh?"

"Yeah. I've always been a crybaby. Sloane would laugh when I finished crying to get me mad or happy or anything but sad. At first, I didn't know what to do with it, but by the third time she did it, I realized I couldn't live without it." Francesca paused and looked at Cecelia. "Thank you. I'm sorry I ruined your afternoon... and possibly your shirt."

"There's nothing to be sorry about."

The effort was appreciated.

Francesca felt slightly uncomfortable with how quickly Cecelia was willing to fit Sloane's role. She shook off that thought and told Cecelia that she should probably take off.

"Maybe we can do this again sometime?" Cecelia asked.

Francesca could only muster a nod. It wasn't a promise, but intent lived behind it.

AFTER GRABBING A TAXI, Francesca headed back to her mother's house. The entire time she went through her conversation with Cecelia. She'd just shared Sloane's biggest secret without hesitation.

Was betraying Sloane all she knew how to do? That wasn't her's to tell; it was Sloane's. Now that Sloane was gone, no one should hear it ever again.

By the time Francesca had slammed the door and paid the cabby, she'd moved past self-flagellation. Anger had taken over. She set her jaw before she stomped in and readied herself.

"Going to start dinner in a few. Needs to simmer," Mama said. Her feet were up on the stacked pallets she'd made into a coffee table, a mystery novel tightly clutched in her fist.

Lines creased Francesca's face.

"That's how you're greeting me? You left me in the plaza! We were supposed to have lunch!"

"Yes. How did it go?"

"After I told you how I was feeling? After I cried about Sloane? We had a great time! We're getting married tomorrow! How do you think it went? I cried about Sloane!"

Mama jumped up and tossed her book aside.

Scurrying across the floor on socked feet, she rushed to Francesca's side. Her face held questions.

"Essie, I had no idea. I thought you could... I don't know. I'm sorry. I'm so sorry. I thought a friend would be good for you."

"A friend? That was a setup!"

"What?" Mama cocked an eyebrow.

Storming past her, Francesca bolted toward the kitchen. "As if you didn't know."

"Didn't know what?"

"Jesus Christ! Cecelia likes me, Mama."

She shrugged. "That's why I thought you'd be good friends."

"Are you kidding me? You didn't know? Really? You *really* didn't?" Like a balloon deflating, Francesca's anger waned.

"Oh, God!" Pale-faced, Mama hesitated before asking, "Essie, is she...?"

"Gay? Yes."

Mama began to cry. She didn't do that often. It had almost always been when she disappointed someone. "I didn't know."

Francesca crushed her in a hug, which her mother returned with such ferocity her back cracked. Since the plane, she'd needed that.

"I believe you. Still, I need to lie down. When dinner is ready, could you bring it to my room?"

"Of course, anything. I really didn't–"

"Could we not?" Francesca shook her head and walked away. "It will be okay. But I need to go be by myself for a while."

Feeling like a zombie, she wanted to leave her arms outstretched, reaching for Sloane's perfume. Maybe it was an okay time to spray it. She should buy a few more bottles. It could be her new scent.

But when she finally reached her temporary room and had her hands wrapped around the tiny glass bottle, she lost her nerve. Pillows and covers called to her. She brought the perfume with her, smelling what she could through the sprayer.

MAMA FUSSED WITH THE ROOM; she dusted around a sleeping Francesca.

"Can't a woman sleep in?"

A spritzer *sst-ed* in the bathroom. "Of course. Don't mind me; I'm just tidying up." The mirror squeaked as Mama wiped off fingerprints Francesca hadn't left.

Yawning, Francesca sat up. "Okay, I'm awake. What activities do we have today?"

"Nothing. This morning is wide open." She opened the curtain, and white light flooded the already bright room.

"And this afternoon?"

Obviously stalling, Mama grabbed a skirt from the floor. "I'll just wash this."

"Mama!"

"Okay, okay! We have dinner with the Loreti's tonight. I didn't know things were going to go poorly yesterday. You can stay home if you want."

Francesca would deal with that in a minute. "And what about this afternoon?"

"I had planned to do some gardening or go for a walk. Maybe sit on the patio and have a nice lunch and talk? Really, Essie; I wanted today to be nothing."

"Oh." The string had finally been pulled on the overhead bulb. "You thought Cecelia and I would be getting lunch or something fun and friendly."

"Well, I'll admit, it had crossed my mind. But that's before I knew; I swear!"

"Calm down. I know. I love the idea of an afternoon on the patio. I have a good book I'd love to catch up on and a day in is very needed. I haven't done this much activity in years. Sloane and I have a calmer life than this." Ribs ached. Oh no: had, not have. It all came back. "Mama, I need you to g–"

She wouldn't. And for the first time, Francesca had someone to hold her as the morning beat her like a hurricane.

12

SLOANE

Mama Nuccio waved her hand towards the center of the table. "Cecelia, could you pass me the salt?"

She had a fish dish in front of her that Sloane didn't recognize.

"Yes, Mama Nuccio," she replied. Who did this woman think she was?

Molly sniffed the air. "Cecelia. Sounds like the name of a harlot."

Sloane was too shocked to say much. She couldn't get the conversation out of her head.

"–sorry. I thought a friend would be good for you."

"A friend? That was a setup!"

Sloane had stopped listening, then.

Mama Nuccio had set Francesca up on a date? She'd thought Mama loved her! Sloane had told her about her given name, even let her call her by it because she'd said, "You have to take it back, Susan. It's your name, not hers." Mama had told her about the letter too.

She and Molly shouldn't have come.

Everyone at the table fit so well as if they were already a

family and had been for ages. And though Sloane had imagined what she would say if they were ever reunited a million times, she wondered if talking to Francesca would only make things worse, make them ache more. Defeated, Sloane started to tell Molly her fears, but wild eyes stared back at her.

"She is off to the powder room. Let us follow her."

Sloane thought to argue, but emotions got in the way. A suctioning feeling took hold of her innards, and she stood right inside the door of a gaudy women's bathroom. The busy purple and gold wallpaper looked like velvet and satin. Sloane took a small moment to lament her lack of touch response while she hovered near a yellow-gold tufted ottoman from the safety of The Gray.

Cecelia strolled in humming a melody softly. The fabric filled bathroom sucked it up as though she were in The Gray too. Sloane watched, transfixed, as Cecelia turned on the faucet. Francesca had become smitten–if only a bit–and Sloane needed to know why.

Cecelia primped in the oversized framed mirror: fluffing dark curled hair, checking pearly teeth. Shifting her weight, red high heels clicked on the onyx marble.

Sloane used her weariness to propel herself forward.

Standing behind Cecelia was strangely intimate. She used to stand behind Francesca and brush her hair aside, kiss her neck. They'd hold each other and stare into the mirror at each other and their future.

The fingerprint smeared replica Venetian 18th century mirror held something different entirely. Alone, Cecelia touched up her gloss as Sloane's grief overcame her. She pictured Francesca's arms around Cecelia's small waist as they stared at each other in a mirror in their new home. So vivid, it felt as if it could be real one day. If it weren't for her being dead already, Sloane's heart would have stopped beating.

A vague reflection of Sloane, barely distinguishable as her, appeared in the mirror above Cecelia's shoulder. As soon as Sloane saw it, she screamed, "What's happening?"

"What are you doing?" Molly snapped. "She was about to see you."

"Was that the plan?" Sloane was shaken.

Molly sighed and became more smoke than girl. "There was no plan. But you had strength you were unable to let yourself tap into. If you cannot give in, how will you be able to contact Francesca one day?"

Sloane's shoulders drooped.

13

FRANCESCA

S he turned the faucet off.

"Rome is a good city to visit. There is certainly plenty to do there," Mama said.

"They have a whole day planned, so we're going to have to leave pretty early. You know that's not my thing. That's why Sloane and I always made things two or three-day trips–so we could leave at eleven or later. We were able to see everything we wanted to, just on a lazier schedule. Mama, I'm not making a mistake; am I?"

Dishes from the evening before and a late breakfast clattered as Mama pulled each out of a soapy water-filled sink. Francesca imagined the pile as a stack of teacups from Alice in Wonderland; if you tugged at the wrong one, they would all crash and shatter.

"No. Alma is a fantastic tour guide! I wish I could be there. I'm proud of you for being able to be around Cecelia." Mama waved her wet dishrag at Francesca. With a smile, she snarked, "Dry faster!"

"Hey! You just got dirty dishwater on me. Thanks, Mama. I really liked this dress."

"I do your laundry. It'll wash. Speaking of dresses, you're already almost out. We'll go shopping later this week."

Leave it to her mother to think Francesca couldn't wear her clothes more than twice. When she was younger, Francesca's wardrobe had been a reasonable size. Wealth had played no part in her life then. Oh, how things had changed.

After another ten minutes of drying, the towel had become too damp to be of any use. Francesca hunched her shoulders in defeat. For some reason, the useless cloth became the end of the world. Eventually, the mood swings had to stop.

"Mama, I need another towel," she said on the verge of tears.

"Go to bed, Essie. There aren't too many more. At least we didn't eat here for dinner, right?" she said. "I'll bring you some wine and chocolate as soon as I'm done; you'll need good sleep for tomorrow."

"No need. I'll be in bed, hopefully already sleeping by then."

Mama's barely lined face creased, as she hedged, "If you're sure..."

Francesca needed to unpack the evening: simple, pleasant conversation with a promise of a trip with the Loreti's. What had she just done?

ALMA WOKE UP TO A MIGRAINE, but Francesca decided to be an adult. She could be around Cecelia—especially with Tony there.

Cecelia had horrible taste in music. Tony complained about it the entire three-hour drive to Rome. Francesca would have preferred resting at such a bleary-eyed hour, but Cecelia had turned Irish wailing to full blast to annoy Tony. Cecelia must be the eldest.

By the time Francesca threw herself out the car, desperate to escape the sibling bickering and melodic noise, she wanted to call and thank Mama for not having any more children.

"So, here we are." Tony beamed. He stretched, and his striped polo lifted up to expose his stomach. As he adjusted his khaki shorts which had become wrinkled and re-tied his hair into a low ponytail, he sighed. "Great, no?"

The siblings called a non-verbal truce the moment they closed the car doors, becoming the adults Francesca knew them to be. Cecelia and Tony led Francesca towards the famous Colosseum. The multi-shades of weathered stone stood hulking above her. She was but an ant in front of the stacked open arches.

"Do you want to take the tour? Or we could just tell you what we know?" Cecelia asked. But when she turned, she must have seen Francesca's wide eyes of wonder as they avoided the lush grass surrounding the broken structure. "Or we could shut up and let you explore. You tell us what you want to do."

"That one," Francesca said–hopefully out loud–as they made their way to the entrance.

Her body hummed with the energy the amphitheatre gave off. She couldn't wait to know more than the blip her World History classes had taught her.

Francesca was thankful she spoke two languages fluently and knew pieces of a few others. It made Italy a whole lot richer; at tourist sites, it made life easier. Cecelia and Tony didn't have to wade through their bits of decent English to ask for tickets or tell the poor harried exchange student named Kelly they wanted the self-guided tour.

"Thank you," Francesca said. Her naked nails, bitten to the quick, clutched her ticket as though it was made of gold and lead to a chocolate factory.

Kelly stood on shaky legs, her blonde hair matted to her head from the hot, windless day. Her eyes read shock as if not a single person in the hour they were open–or maybe since she'd begun working there–had ever thanked her for their ticket.

She stammered, "You're welcome. Hope you enjoy it."

"We will," Francesca assured her with a kind smile. "Hope work goes quickly."

The girl loosened up a little then. "Only five more hours. It's not so bad. It's great pocket change while I'm getting my Bachelors degree."

"Is everything alright?" Cecelia twisted the hem of her tank top.

Clearly, she hadn't been listening at all. Francesca saw Cecelia's face fall when she mentioned Sloane–in English–to Mama at the dinner table the other night, so she knew at least a little of the language. If only she'd paid attention, she could have understood Kelly.

"Yes. I was just chatting with this young lady. She was telling me about her day."

Tony looked utterly lost. "Why?"

"Because. Give me a minute."

Francesca turned back to Kelly, who looked astonished.

"You're Italian is beautiful."

"Thank you. I haven't lived here for a long time, but my mother refuses to use English more than half of the time, so she keeps me on my toes. I'm from San Francisco."

"You're kidding? I'm from LA; what a small world! Anyhow, got to take care of that line."

A line of sixty or so people had built up behind Francesca–each redder than the other.

"Oh! I am so sorry," Francesca said admonishing herself. "Where's your boss? I can explain for you."

"No worries. What's your name?"

"Francesca." She stuck out her hand.

"Nice to meet you, Francesca," Kelly said, shaking it. "And

seriously, no worries; I'm pretty fast. Thanks for chatting. It's been refreshing. Have a great walkthrough. If you end up wanting the tour–" She dropped her voice. "It's on me." Kelly winked.

"Thanks so much." Francesca turned to Cecelia and Tony who looked bored, if not a little irritated. "Ready?"

They nodded. Francesca knew neither Tony nor Cecelia cared about any of this, but the day wasn't about them. Before they made it too far in, Francesca looked behind her. Kelly swiped cards and took cash at breakneck speeds. Just as the line began to dwindle, more people joined it. Luckily, the original angry tourists were filing in quicker than seemed possible.

"Good we got here early."

"Told you so." Tony stuck his tongue out as if he'd dropped twenty years in age.

Francesca nodded and wondered if she would like either of her personal tour guides by the day's end. They yammered on as they entered the expansive circular walkway while Francesca tried to yield what information she could from the leaflet and guides in front of them. Francesca peered over the metal railing meant to keep tourists from jumping into the ruins. The arena itself was a fair distance down, but people have done crazier stunts for photographs.

To think of the blood spilled, the people killed, even the tigers that were slaughtered for the spectator sport of gladiator fighting, made Francesca's stomach turn. All of those lives lost for nothing. Sloane's life lost for nothing. Damn it. How could the rich and royal's enjoyment of the forced struggle of life and death make her think of Sloane?

Because everything did. Francesca found it hard to breathe.

Cecelia touched her shoulder; what coincidental timing. "Are you alright, Francesca? You've been staring into the abyss for a while." She chuckled a little, but worry laced her voice.

"Oh, sorry. I was picturing the violence here. Guess the brochure had me thinking a little morbidly. I'm thinking it's breakfast time. Sorry to cut it short."

"You paid, so why would we care?" Tony said.

"True enough. Well, I should have told you no sad places before I eat." Francesca chuckled. They didn't know her well enough to hear the hollowness behind it.

Cecelia and Tony erupted in laughter.

"Well, Rome's out!" Tony quipped.

"Let's grab something to eat and go to the fountain. It's still early enough it shouldn't be as busy as it would be at say... lunchtime."

Something about the way Cecelia said it had Tony nodding furiously.

RETCHING sounds came from under the bathroom door. Francesca wanted to be supportive from further away, maybe outside in air that smelled of food and perfume, sunscreen and plastic, not Tony's regurgitated stomach contents. Thankfully, Tony told them to leave; he would be there for a bit. He'd call them, he said.

"Are you sure, Tone? We don't mind waiting," Cecelia said. She turned to Francesca and shrugged.

Francesca returned the shrug, wondering which dish he'd eaten had caused his probable food poisoning. "We really don't," she agreed, only gagging a little as she opened her mouth.

"No, no," he said in between heaves. "I'll be fine anytime now. Besides, I have the keys, so I can wait there if I need to. Francesca, I don't want to mess your day up. Please let Cecelia finish your tour; I can't believe this after Mama had to stay home. But we did drive all this way, after all."

How he could so much without vomiting–Francesca didn't know; she was impressed.

"If you're sure..."

"He's sure. Thanks, Tone," Cecelia shouted into the widening space between them and the bathroom as they headed towards the exit.

They left Tony in the bakery to ruin the scent of chocolate pastries for everyone. A few customers had already gone just because of his sounds. Francesca didn't blame them.

A cacophony of tourist guides spiels and squealing birds blared in Francesca's ears as they stepped onto the ancient stone.

Still in a dark state of mind, she wondered what the ground she stood on had seen: the angry chases, bloody fights and deaths by mobs, strolls of love, proposals that lead to bruised knees and kisses. She wished she could witness a moment that would imprint the square, leaving a ghost to haunt the cobblestones forever. Most would be lost to the people in a rush around her, but the street would remember.

Memories of a different kind crashed through her then.

"You okay?" Cecelia asked, too observant for Francesca's liking. "I'm beginning to wonder if today was a good idea."

"Sorry, lost in thought. I haven't been to Italy in a long time," Francesca said.

Too busy attempting to shake out thoughts that would scare all three therapists she'd seen, Francesca couldn't come up with anything better. Usually, she could shake the image of a bloody Sloane wrapped around her when it flitted through her brain. But in squeals of excitement, she heard sirens, and every camera flash had emergency vehicle lights swimming in her vision.

Francesca tilted her head back. Outsiders may assume she enjoyed the radiating sun; reality was, she was hoping her eyes would reabsorb their welling tears.

"Let's carry on with your itinerary; I could use a distraction." Right?

"That, Francesca, we can do. This way!" A grin broke Cecelia's face in two as she laced her fingers with Francesca's and took off running.

Practically being dragged, Francesca's heart exploded with excitement and worry again that she'd made a huge mistake. She hated herself. Hadn't she just been thinking of Sloane's mangled body? Was it okay to live while she grieved? Before she could answer, they were in front of a stone pillar she thought she recognized–its name lost with algebra and the location of a frog's heart.

"Why did we run here?" She was out of shape. "We could see this from the window of the restaurant; I'm sure walking wouldn't have taken all that long."

"True. I just needed the rush." Whoa. Sloane said things like that. "I thought we could wander the square. It wasn't about this monument; it just happened to be a good breather point."

"Right." Francesca dropped Cecelia's hand. "Well, carry on then."

Strappy sandals were a poor choice for a day filled with walking and–apparently–running. Blisters formed by the buckles and at her heels. The back of Francesca's legs felt damp and sticky; she wished she had worn longer shorts.

As they neared a quieter street, she pulled up short. A large fruit stand had become a magnet. Cecelia followed Francesca, despite her initial take-charge lead. The cart blocked their view of the obelisk. Francesca stared at a polished apple, wishing it was shiny enough to see her reflection. Better that she couldn't. She'd see the crease that had begun developing between her eyes almost a year ago.

"I have an idea."

"Oh?" Francesca wasn't sure she was up for 'ideas.'

"Tony and I do this thing where we kiss statues. We have pictures of us doing it since we were teenagers. Silly, I know. But I thought you could join in the tradition. Then, I was going to take you to the Fontana di Trevi–a fun touristy thing. After, we could feed the pigeons. Food would happen at some–"

Francesca hardened her expression. "So we ran around for no real purpose?"

Cecelia looked self-conscious. "I told you; it was to feel alive. Besides, I had to see how you'd handle this before I suggested the statue thing."

"You weren't joking? Cecelia that sounds insane."

"Have I told you I love the way you say my name?"

"Which way?"

"The way you just said it."

"No, I mean which way to the fountain?"

"Oh–" Cecelia looked dejected but held out her hand nonetheless; Francesca did not take it. "This way." Cecelia sighed. "So no kissing statues?"

Francesca chose not to look at Cecelia as she said, "It's not like I can just crawl over hoards of people to kiss a triton."

Despite her irritation at the childish idea, Francesca did like the sparkle in Cecelia's eyes.

"You're right."

They veered towards a smaller street, which Francesca just had to explore. A little fruit kiosk with bright shiny apples sat on the corner. A man stepped out of a modest grocery shop and stood beside the blood oranges. His kind smile made him seem trustworthy–a quality in rare supply.

"I'd like to buy an apple and one other piece that you pick out for me," Francesca said, hoping he owned the fruit stand too.

With an accent so thick she barely understood him, he told her she should go with a cluster of grapes.

They were the freshest thing he had, as a local winery gave him a small sampling of them only two hours before.

They cost a fortune despite her "local" appearance. She couldn't imagine what twelve perfect round purple grapes would cost the tourist couple who had come to browse while she paid. The woman held a small square shopping bag, while the man held three larger ones. She wore a tight 'Bride' tee that stretched over her busty chest, while he wore an equally tight blue tank top with no mention of his marital status.

"Why did you waste your money?" Cecelia asked. "He robbed you blind. I wanted to argue for you, but you pulled out your wallet so quickly it would have been a waste of breath."

"Possibly because it isn't my money; it's Mama's. But more than likely, it's because that apple and I have a connection. Besides, it's a better snack than fried dough." She smirked and added hastily, "Which I still plan to have."

Cecelia cocked one eyebrow and took off towards wherever they were headed. Sloane would have understood the apple connection. Francesca focused on that, not Cecelia's fingertips as they grazed her hand at an unnatural angle now and again as they moved in tandem towards the Trevi Fountain.

She tried desperately not to glance sideways. The one time she did, Cecelia's lacy bra had peeked out from under her loose top. Francesca had not expected ever again to feel the stirring the indigo fabric brought on.

She groped for Sloane's face. Her current feeling, coupled with the image of Sloane's fire hair and green eyes, blonde eyebrows and pale lips, had a visceral memory of Sloane's taste entering her mind.

A noise nearly escaped Francesca as she recalled the sounds Sloane would make as she painted swirls inside of her. She rubbed her thumb on her palm as Sloane often did. Something was comforting about the endearing motion, but also erotic.

Usually, that touch led to Sloane running her fingers along Francesca's arms slowly. She'd pause at the soft spot at the crook of her arm; Francesca always moaned at the seemingly un-erogenous zone. Fingertips would trace her collarbone, walking their way down to her wanting breasts.

A sharp pain rippled through Francesca's toe as she ran into a small kiosk in the middle of the square. Cecelia spun around to catch her, despite her lack of falling. Their breasts grazed each other, and chills ran down Francesca's spine. She gasped. In an attempt to cover it, she shouted, "Ouch!" Her mind spun, and she reminded herself that Sloane, not Cecelia, had her worked up. Francesca wanted to create a mantra about that to ease the knot forming in her stomach, but Cecelia was already talking to her.

"–not the day I'd hoped. Are you okay?"

Francesca thought to laugh. "It'll sting for a bit, but I'll be fine. Speaking of, should we check on Tony?"

"He's a big boy. He'll be okay. We'll call him before lunch."

Could it be lunch yet?

"That sounds good. Where could a girl get some fried dough around here?"

"What happened to this apple being a good snack?" Cecelia bit into it for emphasis. The crisp sound of the skin breaking seemed louder than the newly wedded couple's exclamations about being over-charged. Apple juices dribbled down Cecelia's plump lips, and Francesca frantically looked around for relief.

Finding one, her voice echoed down the thin corridor. "Look! A snack!"

"What? That butcher shop?"

On the window, a smiling pig had a pitchfork through his stomach. The awning above the shop read, 'Meat'. A large picture window gave passersby an in-depth look into the life of a butcher. No hidden, backroom chopping and tearing down for 'Meat'.

"They may have sandwiches, and I could go for a sandwich."

"If you're that hungry, let's go to a restaurant. We could get a real lunch," Cecelia said. She'd stopped walking to stare intensely into Francesca's eyes as if she were about to say, 'I love you'.

"Not that hungry, but I couldn't finish breakfast." Tony's gagging had turned her stomach. "Still, I need a little something to tide me over until lunch," Francesca said. Her gaze squirmed away, and her irritation began to rise. "And you just ate my apple."

"Do you want me to get you another one? I can do that while you check out the butcher shop. Or we could find something along the way?"

Francesca agreed. Her nerves had calmed her sex drive so she felt she could handle more alone time with Cecelia, but a few minutes apart would still do her some good. After all, she had been excited about Sloane, not Cecelia. Cecelia would only be a cheap replacement for Sloane. Francesca was having to remind herself of that often.

THEIR ARMS HAD INCHED BACK towards each other some time during the day, hands grazing now and again.

By the time Francesca could see the parking lot, both elation and self-loathing consumed her brain like a Celtic knot. Francesca decided the only way to keep anything from happening was avoidance, but she hadn't decided if she wanted that yet.

"Looks like Tone made it to the car alright." Cecelia pointed to the long dark hair plastered against the interior of the car window. "Told you he'd be fine."

Hours he'd been there, yet she seemed so blasé about it. Maybe he got sick often and ended up hanging out in cars more often than the average person. It's not as if there was a 'type' for that kind of thing.

"Yeah. He's asleep at least," Francesca said, hoping her voice wasn't as guilty as her conscious.

Cecelia stopped short of the car and turned, her face flushed from heat and hours worth of skin brushing skin. "I had an amazing day," she commented, testing Francesca's resolve.

Francesca probably matched pink for pink. "Me too. Thank you for showing me Rome. It was–" She searched for a word. "–different than I remember."

Disappointment shadowed Cecelia's face; Francesca's hesitation must have signaled something she hadn't meant it to.

"How so?" she asked quietly.

"Well, I remembered it being stuffier. I truly appreciate you taking me to the Musei Vaticani."

Francesca wished she could say more, stop being so short with what she said, but conversations felt too much like opening up as of late.

"I've driven to Rome to wander through the Sistine Chapel, so I completely understand. The Vatican is a holy place; sometimes you just have to breathe that in." Cecelia smiled and reached for Francesca's hand.

As if she were a small animal in the woods, Francesca didn't move as the wavy-haired hunter grew ever closer. Her heart tried to rip through her chest while she decided if she would run or embrace the bullet.

Cecelia took a step forward.

"Yes, very holy," Francesca said, grasping for words.

Closing her eyes, Cecelia leaned forward. Her full lips separated ever so slightly. Francesca held her breath. With a feather's worth of space between them, a small flock of pigeons cooed loudly and flew up in a swoop of grey and white. Francesca's heart did a flip-flop, and her eyes flicked towards the racket. She stepped back. Gravel crunched under her sandals.

Cecelia's eyes squinted before they opened, and a sad sigh escaped her lips before they closed and retreated. Silently, she strolled towards the driver side and knocked on the glass. It took four hard knocks before Tony woke up.

Francesca wondered if she should stand there, one step away from kissing Cecelia, or head to the car, miles away from kissing Cecelia.

Tony rolled the window down. On the drowsy side of alert, he questioned, "You coming, Francesca? Hurry up and close the door. It's so hot!" He had no idea.

"Coming."

Though he'd had the air conditioning on, it came out forced, dry and angry, warm and suffocating. Francesca should have walked home. It would have only taken, what? A few days at her pace?

Holding onto both seats, twisted like a pretzel, Tony turned to Francesca. "So, how was the day? Sorry I missed it!" The left side of his face had a seatbelt indention and a line of drool. He wiped it away and rubbed the slime on his khaki shorts. "I feel much better now. Want to stop for a late gelato and dinner? I know you two worked up an appetite running about Rome for... what? Eight hours, or so?"

Cecelia didn't respond. She just put the car in reverse and started driving away.

"Sounds about right," Francesca said. Tony hadn't done anything, so she tried to keep it natural between them. "And I'm up for dinner."

Dark eyes and thick eyelashes flicked towards her in the rearview mirror. They narrowed. It pissed Francesca off.

She hadn't made the flock of pigeons go nuts; she hadn't ruined the moment, and neither had Tony. He needed to eat after a horrible day in the car.

"Great!" His head swiveled to Cecelia. He was right by her ear. "Cecelia, where do you want to go?"

"Home. I'm too tired. You two can go eat after you drop me off."

"I can't wait three hours. I was sick!" Tony emphasized the 'sick' with an inflection matching no emotion Francesca knew.

Cecelia sighed.

"And I can appreciate that. You getting sick was bad and all, but it doesn't matter. I still want to go home."

Tony plopped back in his seat with a muffled sigh. "Home it is then."

14

SLOANE

For Sloane, no word could describe the prospect of touching Francesca again. Though she knew she shouldn't get her hopes up, a little glowing ball of it still grew in her chest.

"Okay," Sloane muttered as she began to focus on the night that had ended her, had ended everything: their six-year anniversary. Sloane could hardly believe it had been so long, yet she felt she'd known Francesca forever.

Sloane hadn't wanted to wait to pop the question, but Francesca had told her they didn't need to get married; it didn't make a difference.

"You'll always be mine, without a doubt." Francesca would say, whenever she brought it up.

Sloane didn't care; Francesca was going to marry her.

They had arrived at Francesca's favorite diner late because she hadn't been able to decide which dress to wear for dancing. "I want to look perfect, Sloane. Six years is a huge deal. We'll want to take a hundred pictures, of course."

"But we'll forget to take more than a few at the beginning,

because we're so caught up, just like every year," Sloane had reminded her, a smile spreading across her lips.

She'd stood behind Francesca–once again in awe of her beauty and her luck–as Francesca had tugged at her slinky red and black geometric patterned dress. Their full-length mirror hung on the back of the closet door they left open to pretend they had a wardrobe. It barely fit Francesca's dresses.

"Not this year, we have to do better. We don't have enough pictures of us lately. We will take some side by side at dinner and make sure we ask people to take pictures of us dancing too."

Francesca had slid her dangly coral earrings in and stared meaningfully at Sloane in the mirror, adding a wink for emphasis.

"Of course, baby, whatever you want. The salsa club has terrible lighting, though. We can have ice cream after and take photos there."

"I hate this dress," Francesca had muttered.

Before Sloane could stop her, Francesca had stripped, tossed the dress behind her, and grabbed a lace dress with the tags still on she'd been saving for "the right occasion".

Sloane had decided on a turquoise maxi dress with paint splatter white hibiscus flowers before deciding on the evening's activities. It wasn't flashy, but Francesca had always purred when she slipped it on. Sloane'd wanted to give her a night she'd love before they ended up in what would forever be "their spot," so a purr was a good sign.

Sloane's eyes had lit up as Francesca spun around and shifted her hair over her shoulder. "Oh, my love," Sloane had gasped. "You look beautiful."

The cream of the cap-sleeve dress brought out the tan of her skin and stood in stark contrast to her near-black hair. So striking, Sloane had hesitated. "We could stay in?" she'd joked. Even if Francesca had agreed, Sloane had plans.

"Love, we're going. Now, it's your turn," Francesca had said. "Take my breath away."

And Sloane had, when she died. But that had been then.

SLOANE'S LUNGS burned as The Gray ripped her to a parking lot. To her right stood something she and Francesca had sworn they'd see together one day: the Colosseum. To her left, rows and rows of parked cars filled with luggage awaiting visitors' return. But betrayal stood right in front of her.

Cecelia was leaning into Francesca like the hussy she was. And Francesca stood there waiting with such anticipation she'd been struck still.

Molly gasped as The Gray rippled around them. Unlike the hole Sloane had torn through the other side, any shifting she'd caused then was from rage. Her anger had Molly clasping her hand over her mouth. She was shocked Francesca couldn't feel it too. The pigeons did; as if Sloane had charged at them, they dispersed with vigor. The flock flew up chaotically, desperate to escape the enmity.

Sloane spun around, unable to face Francesca moving on.

In such a small voice, it was almost lost, Molly told her, "She pulled back".

To crumple or not to crumple? "It doesn't matter," Sloane said through a tight jaw.

It took Molly a moment to respond. She watched Francesca watching Cecelia. Curiosity almost had questions coming from Sloane's lips, but she held them. Her fists were tight, and she hated that she could feel her nails cut into her palms.

Being dead should hurt less.

"I need to be anywhere but here," Sloane barely said.

Hectic thoughts raced through her mind.

Fights, makeup sex, promises to never have makeup sex again, Thanksgiving traditions, a trip to the Grand Canyon.

With nausea she shouldn't have to have in The Gray, Sloane was sucked away to a full square. It matched her chaotic mood. "Where are we?" she questioned Molly, who hovered beside her.

Molly shrugged. "You chose this location. I only followed you here."

A bewildered Sloane swiveled her head. "I didn't, though. My thoughts were too jumbled to pick a place; I just needed to get away."

"Well, we are away," snarked the irritating peasant girl. No, it wasn't Molly's fault Sloane felt empty.

They wandered through the crowds, through the living: the natives and tourists, adults and children in search of a landmark. Without warning, as if caught in a flytrap, she became stuck inside of a woman with large clogs and a short patterned red dress. She pulled up short and stood still with Sloane inside of her.

Their thoughts mingled as if they'd become one person. Sloane could hear her thinking about her useless boyfriend and how she'd dump him as soon as they got home. The woman hoped she could wear him out with sightseeing so they wouldn't have to have any more sex. It wasn't terrible, but he got too sweaty.

Sloane's thoughts on how weird it felt to be living snuck in, which confounded the woman. She followed the idea with her own of how being a ghost may be 'cool'.

With serious effort, Sloane mustered the energy to step out of the nameless, unsatisfied woman. Speechless, the woman seemed no worse for the wear. Sloane watched the woman acknowledge the man who'd brought her a bottle of water.

"Here you go, babe," he said with a smile that read, 'I want to marry you.'

"K, thanks," she replied with no interest at all. Her eyes weren't even looking in his direction; they were checking out a GQ model practically running through the square.

"What the hell was that?" Sloane asked aloud. Could this day get any worse?

"You are much quicker than I had expected, especially considering your lack of ability to interact with the living in other ways." Molly's compliment took the sting away from the insult, as intended. "You body-melded. My first time was an accident, as well."

"Okay, so you can do it too..." Sloane wasn't sure if that made it better or worse.

Nodding, Molly sighed, "Yes, but I do wish I knew more about it. Much is still unknown to me, and I am unable to do much while I'm in another person."

Sloane had so many questions. "Can I move with them?"

Molly tightened her clasped hands. "Yes. It will take some time, and it does not last long, but you can."

"Can I body-meld with *anyone*?"

15

FRANCESCA

Strands of red tickled Francesca's collarbone. The weight of Sloane's head made her breathing shallow but satisfying. She stirred but didn't wake up until Francesca began stroking her hair.

"Hm?" she murmured sleepily.

Yellow light streamed in through the cracks of the curtains. Particles from dusty books glittered above them as if life was an art film with everything perfectly framed and expertly angled. Even Sloane's face seemed flushed just so.

Lucky didn't cover it.

"How long have you been awake?" Sloane asked as she slid across Francesca and pulled herself up to meet her face. She sighed, probably because of the chilly pillow–she loved that.

"Long enough." Francesca kissed her sticky forehead. "You don't have to wake up."

A dimple formed on her cheek. "I do. I need to tell you something that's very important."

Francesca leaned forward. Their lips touched so lightly it wasn't enough. They became greedy. Sloane pulled her close and kissed her as only she could. When she pulled back, they were gasping.

"I still need to tell you something."

Francesca took a deep breath. "Is it a good thing?"

"The best." Sloane cupped her cold and clammy hand on Francesca's cheek.

"Okay." She leaned into it and stared into Sloane's emerald eyes, flecks of gold danced as she tried not to blink.

"I'll be with you soon," she said. "I need you to wait for me."

Before Francesca had a chance to question what her lover meant, Sloane began fading away. She tried to grab her hand, hold on to her forever, but she just felt her own cheek.

"You can't leave me," Francesca whispered to the dusty nothingness.

Her mouth still formed the word "me," and her hand was still resting on her cheek when she woke with dried tears on her face.

Sloane was dead; Francesca's chest shook as it came back in waves.

The smell of pink and strawberries swirled in the room—a fleeting memory. Touching her lips, Francesca jerked up from the mounds of tangled sheets. Sloane's glass strawberry sat on the chair with its cap off. An open book lay beside it.

Standing felt nearly impossible, but the bed offered a haven she didn't deserve.

After Tony and Cecelia had dropped her off, she'd rushed in and had dinner with Mama. Mama knew. Somehow, she knew something had happened. Silence could have been an indicator. Or it could have been the solemn, disappointed look Francesca's face held. Mama didn't ask about the trip, only if Francesca wanted seconds of her ravioli. She didn't.

"I'm turning in a little early," Francesca had said.

Mama had just nodded and said she loved her.

Francesca only remembered tears and pain. Sloane was her once-in-a-lifetime love, and she had been there with Cecelia. If it weren't for those pigeons–if it weren't for those pigeons, what? Would she have let Cecelia's lips touch hers? Would she have kissed her back? Yes.

Betrayer.

Francesca cried for Sloane, not for herself. She didn't remember opening Sloane's perfume, though. But she must have. She didn't remember opening a book. But she must have. So, she stood to see what her grief-drunken-self had left for her hungover-self.

Before she looked at the book, she capped the perfume. Having wasted enough already, she couldn't bear to lose more. She clung to it like a child to a stuffed animal as she looked at the book. It was an obscure book she'd forgotten she'd brought from Sloane's side table. On the open page, words and phrases were circled. "Be back, wait, love."

Sloane's perfume bottle slipped from Francesca's hands. To catch it, she hit her knee on a small knot in the wood and slid a little on the uneven floor. Her knee throbbed. Looking down, she saw reddened skin. Francesca stared at the forming bruise and lost time. She put the perfume back in her suitcase and rubbed burning eyes that had nothing to do with her knee.

The only sound Francesca heard throughout the house was Mama's slight snore. Whatever time it was, the sun's glow barely peeked over the horizon. Taking advantage of the alone time, Francesca took the book with her out into the tiny garden. She read aloud from the page with the circled words.

"Sloane, if you're there... God, I haven't done this in ages." Francesca continued to read. She didn't understand it. She hardened her resolve. "Sloane, if you're there, give me a sign. I need you. I'm so sorry."

Tears made her reading sporadic and pointless after that.

Mama came out during the third chapter. "Oh, Essie!"

"It was only a dream," Francesca cried softly, wet cheeks trembling as she said it.

"Let's get you inside."

As she shakily stood and hobbled in to eat the inevitable breakfast Mama would fix for her, Francesca made a decision she knew would be unpopular. She waited until after they'd finished a nice meal, until after they'd gotten ready for the day, until after Mama had asked what she wanted to do for the day.

Francesca stared at a blue tile below her swollen knee. "I'm going to go home."

Mama blinked. "Are you serious?" She must have believed her at least a little because she didn't laugh or ignore her.

"Yes." More serious than she had been about anything except for loving Sloane.

"Essie, no! Not now; now you need to be with Mama," she said without her usual vigor. She knew it wasn't a battle worth fighting. Still, it seemed she couldn't help but go through the motions.

Unable to deal, Mama cleaned. She grabbed their plates and shuffled over to the trash can to scrape off crumbs. The scrape of the fork on porcelain filled the large kitchen and made Francesca's eardrums wince. Mama took the plates to the sink and scoured them as though they were casserole dishes with cheese caked on, while there had only been a tiny smear or two of jam from their overstuffed biscuits. Drying the plates took nearly as long as the washing.

Francesca wouldn't wait for Mama to wipe down the counters with three kinds of cleaners, then sweep and mop the floor. She was just going home.

"Mama..."

Making the dishes an art form, Mama made an exceptional amount of noise as she put the two plates and butterknife away.

Francesca could have filmed it, put a horror soundtrack behind it, and what a short it would be. The tension would have had an audience on the edge of their seat.

"Mama, look, I need to go through my apartment. If I decide to move here–" Mama stopped soaping the island. "I'll need my things. It's been a wonderful vacation, but real life is telling me I need to get my shit together. I need to make decisions that are a little less bohemian."

Sloane would have been fine living out of a pretty much useless suitcase. And if it weren't for the lack of Sloane, the lack of pictures of Sloane, and Cecelia, Francesca may be preparing for another adventure filled day.

"It's because of Rome isn't it?"

Francesca's eyes sprouted a leak as she inspected a soap glob in the sink.

"You should be with someone, not alone; Susan wouldn't want that."

"Stop! Stop pretending what you want is what Sloane would want. She would want me to figure my shit out my own way; she would want me to be happy. And you know what? She'd want to be here."

As if she'd said nothing, Mama continued, "Let Mama help. You could live here, or I could help you find a place. Just don't go back."

"Mama, stop." Francesca saw the letter in time to move. "No, not this time."

Her mother stopped moving for a second and nodded. "Fine. But you come back. This is your home now."

16

FRANCESCA

Wrinkled grey sheets awaited Francesca's exhausted body. Stained and reeking of grief, she slept in her reading chair.

Though she'd sweated all night, she couldn't take off the Sloane-scented blanket she'd wrapped around herself. By the morning, airport-smell clung to it.

She woke to the morning light streaming in through their curtains as it had in her dream. All she could think to do was curl her knees to her chest while heaves cracked her ribs.

Francesca lost that first day just as she'd lost the first month. With spiraling maudlin thoughts it was as though the last two weeks hadn't happened. She slid back into the routine of falling apart every moment she spent in the apartment. Unlike before, she had no reason to leave. With no job, no friends, no family, she just stayed in a state of *apart*. She deserved it, though, didn't she?

Mama called. Francesca must have answered because she didn't call again for a few days. They could have talked about pink elephants or blowing up a hospital–she'd dreamt about both within the past week–Francesca couldn't recall.

17

ONE YEAR

Francesca stopped breathing.

Sloane had been snatched from her exactly one year ago. Francesca had tried not to keep track; she thought it morbid and unhealthy.

Her heart seized at the moment the accident happened as if her body was having a memory. Francesca lay on the floor curled up imagining a dead Sloane wrapped around her as the sights and sounds rushed back, real and tangible. She held her breath waiting for the ambulance.

18

FRANCESCA

She was nothing.

19

FRANCESCA

Her lips cracked, and the sink seemed impossibly far away.

20

FRANCESCA

She crawled across the boxy room and used the refrigerator handle to tug herself vertical.

FRANCESCA

She ate an expired breakfast bar and halfway changed the sheets.

Shortly after, another wave of grief hit. Bits of granola and cranberries burned her throat as they came up as solid as when she'd eaten them.

SLOANE

S loane shouldn't have followed Francesca.

Hot tears dripped down her nose as she prayed The Gray would swallow her whole—unfair she could still cry in The Gray. Molly had let her go alone.

Sloane had intended for her sobs to echo through the space surrounding Francesca in hopes Francesca would feel Sloane's presence. She didn't, though; she held it in. Sloane had to let Francesca go.

If anyone had asked her when she was alive, she would have said if either of them died the other would follow with a broken heart. But Francesca hadn't; she'd picked herself up and been able to breathe again.

Was Sloane trying to take that away from her? She'd thought she'd be bringing them back together, bringing Francesca peace. At the moment, she didn't know what to think.

Sloane pictured her arms around Francesca. Fear kept her planted in the corner, a voyeur in her own home, wondering if her whole endeavor was selfish. Francesca had had fleeting moments of happiness in Italy. Would she be taking those away?

Though it shredded Sloane to see Francesca laugh, it also warmed her. She wasn't laughing now; she couldn't.

Sloane should tell Molly she was done; she had to let Francesca heal.

"Are you ready to leave this place?" Molly asked, appearing from The Gray on the sixth day. "You have watched long enough."

"Am I being selfish?"

"Perhaps," Molly replied without missing a beat as if she were omniscient. She scrunched her small face and put her hand on her plainly dressed hip. "But would Francesca not be selfish as well?"

23

FRANCESCA

On the seventh day home, Francesca crawled out of the hole she'd fallen in. The second tasteless breakfast bar staying down had to be a sign. Of what, she wasn't sure.

She started small: a too-hot shower that washed away her still free-flowing tears. The bathroom light wasn't her friend, but the mirror she tried to ignore revealed a face so puffy her freckles were ink blots. Francesca hadn't been surprised; her face felt so tight, she wondered how her skin hadn't split open. Exposed muscles would have been deserved. She'd lived; Sloane hadn't.

After, Francesca laid on the bed, wet and wrapped in one of Sloane's t-shirts. She called Mama to tell her that she hadn't died. The deja vu of it hit her hard, but she shook it off.

"Hi," she croaked through a raw and bloodied throat.

"Essie! It's so good to hear your voice. I've already found you a few houses to look at. Just check your email when you can. If you like one, I'll tell them to put it on hold. Everyone knows me, of course, and knows you may be moving here. They all love the idea. So all you have to do is say yes, and one thing's off the list.

As for packing and moving, I can hire someone; I'll pay for it too. You'll pick what to keep or not to. If you don't want to do that now, they can pack it all, and you can do that later."

Leave it to her mother to take care of it all for her. Almost three weeks ago, Mama had been the same windstorm. Part of Francesca wanted to hang up; the other wanted to thank her.

"I just called to let you know I wasn't dead, but I'll check my email and call you back tomorrow."

It had been ages since she'd been on a computer. With no friends to keep in touch with and no Sloane to photograph, what would have been the point? Her life in San Francisco had become rib-shattering grief, therapy attempts, and notes to herself about eating.

Francesca's bruised knee throbbed as she walked to the small rolling wooden desk shoved half in their never-closed closet. The drawer squealed as Francesca rolled it out, and her heart sped up. A photograph of Sloane laughing was on top of a stack of envelopes under the laptop. Squeezing her eyes closed, she grabbed the old laptop covered in stickers.

She slammed the drawer shut on the memory behind it and tried to steady her breathing and ignore the desire to cry. Opening her dusty laptop made her feel like an alien. As it was nearly midnight, the screen light tired her already sore eyes. Wearily, she began to go through her emails.

The monotony of it reminded her of Sloane making fun of her for being glued to her computer. Junk mail filled her inbox; she spent over two hours weeding through it all. Finally, by 3 am, she stared at the listings Mama had sent with a cocktail of dread and anticipation.

The first one had no real view and needed too much work for Francesca's emotional state. She pictured herself ripping out cabinets, outside weeding on knee pads, scrubbing the tile grout and became overwhelmed. Besides, the price tag almost made her lips twitch. Francesca would have been okay in a carbon copy of her current shoebox. Perhaps she would prefer it.

But nothing like that was a choice. Five emails later, she found a home reminiscent of Mama's villa—view and all, but it came with a twenty-acre vineyard. What Francesca would do with that was beyond her, but she could figure that out later. Maybe she'd open up a winery. With that ludicrous thought in mind, Francesca blearily dialed her mother's number.

"I knew you'd love their place!" Mama squealed. "They said they are willing to do some customizations before you move in too! I'll send you a list. We can go over all of that tomorrow. I know it's very late. You call me tomorrow—whenever is fine. I don't mind waking up early for this! I'm so very excited for you. Susan wou—"

"Mama," Francesca cut her short. She grabbed her laptop and headed back towards the beckoning bed. "So, how much does this place cost?"

"It's reasonable. Don't you worry. Narcissa and I talked about it and came to a good price."

"And that is?"

Francesca flipped on a small shadeless lamp beside her bed. Just a wooden base and bulb, it filled the room with light. That should keep her awake long enough to read about the customizations. She wanted it done with. In some ways, she could be described as excited, in most, resigned to a life away from Sloane's memories.

"Don't you worry your beautiful head about that. I've already got the money. I'm buying it. You keep saving your savings."

Too stunned and choked up to argue, Francesca simply said, "I love you."

"I love you too, Essie. I'll email you the list now, and talk to you tomorrow. I'll get lists of movers and wire you the money in a few hours. By the time you wake up, everything will be done.

And don't worry about the dual-citizenship situation; you already have it. Don't know if I ever told you that or if you even thought that far ahead." Mama paused. "You can apply for an ancestral passport once you're all settled for added proof, though."

Francesca nodded, so moved by Mama's generosity. Though she couldn't see it, Francesca hoped she felt it.

"Talk to you soon, Essie. I'm beyond thrilled."

"You're the best mom," Francesca said to no one, as Mama had hung up to go finish organizing her daughter's new life.

As she rubbed her watering eyes, Francesca imagined Sloane's weight next to her so solidly she would have sworn there'd been an indention. The feeling had her closing her laptop and switching off the light. She'd deal with it in the morning after all.

"Goodnight," Francesca said despite herself.

The bed sheets shifted, and she let her quiet sobs carry her into darkness.

"Easy, easy!" she said for the hundredth time, as her hands flew out in front of her again. Francesca had had a chance to pack up most of the small duds in the days after she chose the villa, but the medium and big things were beyond her time and energy.

During the fastest moving process ever, Francesca lived with a massive lump of guilt in her chest. With each rip of tape and squeak of a marker on the packed boxes, Francesca worried more and more, but less and less.

The teenage mover who'd come with his dad was a bit clumsy. As he grabbed pictures off the wall and breakable lamps with the care of a toddler, Francesca had to remind him they weren't plastic do-dads; they were irreplaceable memories.

In a way, she thought to thank him. Her anxiety over her worldly possessions getting broken had her swallowing her tears during the day. The one thing she'd trade it all in for had been taken from her. Francesca wished keeping all of Sloane's worldly possessions could fill the emptiness.

When she stumbled on a half-filled-in sudoku, she knew it would stay unfinished on the bookshelf sandwiched in between priceless antique books and paranormal romance novels. The only things she threw away were the foul-smelling food in the refrigerator, freezer meals covered in icicles, and an expired bag of chips she found under the bed.

As the movers bagged jackets Sloane had collected from every city she'd visited as if they were trash, she stared at her feet to keep from screaming. Tears dripped onto the old towels lying on the floor to keep the men's boots from scuffing the wood.

The book-lined walls were the most painful. Sloane's carefully chosen books had been tucked in nooks and crannies, on bookshelves, and stacked on the floor as if a library had gone out of business, and the librarian who'd taken the books home had suddenly become homeless. The environment had been Sloane's sanctuary. It pained Francesca to see them tossed in a box like old toys. She told the movers to pack each shelf together, but they'd only half-listened.

As she'd expected that, Francesca had photographed the apartment. She'd be able to recreate it in her new house no matter how they were boxed and shipped. In a new environment, their library wouldn't make her cry; she'd only feel joy that Sloane would be with her always. Right?

When the sky could be no darker, the movers stood awkwardly on the smallest piece of concrete anyone could still call a front stoop. A place their size shouldn't have taken so long, they probably figured. However, Francesca knew they were being paid well. Mama always saw to that, having been a working mother for so long.

The eldest mover, practically holding a newsboy cap to his chest in all of his earnestness, stared at her with a sad smile. "That's it, ma'am. We'll lock these up tight, so in the morning the truck can come hitch it on. It'll fly out within a day or two. That's up to the pod company."

Francesca hadn't made the arrangements; she wasn't even sure what pod company they were using. Her brain felt like the violently smashed egg in the 90s drug commercial, so she didn't ask.

She pulled her hair into a puffed-up bun.

"Okay, thank you," she said, hoping she looked less dazed than she felt.

"Sorry about the mess," he continued after an uncomfortable silence. Despite their completely regular clothing, something about the two felt out of place in San Francisco, as if they were passing through on their way to some ghost mining town in Oregon.

"Good luck, and travel safe," the kid with an unexpectedly baritone voice crooned. Only having grunted until then, Francesca had begun to wonder if he was mute.

Francesca shook his hand firmly. His weak handshake strengthened to match, and he stood a little straighter. "Thanks," she said. "Stay good."

They left her with only a suitcase filled with who-knows-which clothes, an odd assortment of toiletries, and a sleeping bag to say goodbye to Sloane's home.

She slept beside the flammable synthetic feather-stuffed cocoon on the hardwood floor. Being uncomfortable seemed fitting. It would be her last opportunity to fall apart in their home. She spent the night regretting her decision and telling

Sloane she was sorry until her mouth could no longer formulate words.

When she woke, she found her crusted cheek stuck on the toilet seat, her knees felt bruised from being at an odd angle all night, and her right hand had fallen into the–thankfully–clean water. Sometime between then and the morning, she'd seen her way to the bathroom. She had little memory of anything but the sorries she'd said into the dark. Seeing vomit stuck to her cheek had her thinking about her short-lived party days. She had the same sickly pallor with matted hair and bloodshot eyes. Tacky times at tacky high.

"Italy is for the best," she assured the mirror as she scrubbed her toilet-waterlogged hands with a hotel bar of soap from her 'overnight bag'. Once her hands were ruby red, she took a long shower.

Her flight was at 4:45 pm, and it was only noon. She had time to waste and no loose ends to tie up, no goodbyes to say. Other than a doctor or two, the only person Francesca kept in contact with was the landlord. He told her to leave the keys under the mat and to have a great life. Though he cared enough to send a card around Christmas time, it wasn't enough for a hug as she moved away for good. Francesca grasped at the image of his face. Blonde hair and a medium build came to her. A blurry face and a muddled voice followed. Well, it seemed she wouldn't miss him much either.

Francesca's empty stomach growled: a task to complete. She headed to a sandwich shop she and Sloane used to frequent. When she entered through the smudgy glass doors that swung closed too quickly, it felt so familiar. The same young woman with dreads had waited tables there for the past three years. When Francesca and Sloane came in, she'd acknowledge them by name and food order. They'd breeze over their weeks in two sentences or less, and she'd move on to the next table of regulars: superficial, but comforting.

"Hi Francesca," she said. Her honey perfume filled Francesca's nostrils. "Long time. How are you?" Her light brown brows pulled together tightly.

"Good, thanks."

"No, seriously."

"I can't, April. I'm moving away today and talking–" Francesca's voice broke.

Ripped nails grasped the table as she leaned forward. "Moving? Where?"

"Italy. Well, at least for the moment."

"I hope it's better for you. I hope you get some peace there. You deserve it."

She leaned in for the first contact they'd ever made. Francesca almost heaved on her shoulders but stopped herself with a cough.

After untangling her arm from the strips of frayed fabric that made up the world's most complicated shirt, Francesca forced a smile.

"You'll be missed," she said as she left a check on a booth with a loud blonde woman, three matching children, and a stoic dark-haired man with a splotchy red face.

When the Reuben sandwich arrived–cold with a side of soggy–Francesca ate slowly.

The food didn't taste as good as it used to. Each bite brought with it another thin film of grease until Francesca's mouth stopped recognizing anything but oil and a vague hint of perfume she couldn't shake. All that before she made it to the over-fried frozen potatoes.

Hoping it would de-grease her mouth, she went for a fry. As if a lightning fast wind blew through, her water tipped into the red basket soaking the checkered paper and already soggy steak fries. If she had looked away for a second, she would have guessed someone had knocked it over. But, she hadn't.

"Sloane?" she whispered as she whipped her head around. It had to be her; Francesca was tired of pretending she wasn't there with her often. Before she'd even thought to dry the table, Francesca dialed Mama.

"Did you buy the villa already?"

"We're still tidying things up."

"But did you pay for anything yet?"

Mama's worry was a thread sewn through her words. "Essie, what is this about?"

"I need you to stop. I want to look when I'm there. I need to feel the place."

Mama took a deep breath. "We've gone through this already. Your stuff is being delivered there. It may take a few days to get adjusted, but once we unpack and organize, you'll feel more at home. You're just getting nervous."

"No, Mama. I need to pick the place myself. I know it sounds crazy, but I think–" There was a pregnant pause. "I think it's what Sloane would want."

A second longer silence followed. Francesca itched to speak, just to break the tension, but she'd said all she needed.

"Essie, I understand. If it's your heart–if this is about Susan– we will pick a place out when you arrive. You aren't moving to get away from her after all, and I know how soon it is. I'll call them in the morning. I love you, Essie. Make it here safely."

"I love you too, Mama."

Francesca hung up breathing easier than she had in weeks.

24

SLOANE

S loane squirmed.

"Be still," Molly said. "Else they may feel you."

A scratchy voice overhead muffled Molly's next sentence. "The seatbelt sign is on."

"It's so weird. The guy's dreaming about his boss. It's a bit lewd. Yeah, we'll go with lewd. And not in a way you'd expect." Sloane realized as a child she probably had no idea what to expect.

"You will learn to block it out, I promise. It just takes time, just as it will take time to control their voice and move in their skin. I cannot remember how long it took me. Years, maybe a century?"

Sloane decided not to unpack that.

Francesca sat near the middle of the large plane. Sloane was one row behind and to the right of her inside of a slim man wearing a grey fitted business suit and a bright purple pocket square. He felt rich, self-important. Sloane just saw him as a body to meld with who had too many dreams and poor taste in music.

She popped out of him and tore his earbuds out of his

goofily large ears, before sliding back in with ease. Though only her fourth attempt, she'd already begun handling body-melding well.

Mind free of one nuisance, Sloane strained to hear Francesca. But she seemed to be in her 'ignore people and listen to the extensive music library stored on her laptop' mood.

Aside from in-flight movies and one man in the back with horrible sleep apnea, the plane was relatively quiet. No one chatted with their partners or busied themselves in their seat-mates lives; they all kept to themselves. It gave Sloane time to think, which she didn't want. Molly had suggested they "fly with Francesca" to hear her conversations. To Sloane, it was a way to see how she was doing. Would she want to do that anymore after Francesca settled in Italy?

The "deathiversary," as Molly called it, had come and gone. Sloane had spent the first few days curled around Francesca's grief-stricken figure. She'd matched her tear for tear while slipping into utter loneliness again as if they'd hit rewind to Francesca's homecoming from the hospital. She'd been unable to move, unable to function. Sloane had laid beside her, a knot of pain settling deep.

A year later and Sloane still couldn't escape The Gray. Every step forward felt like a waste, though. Able to do what she could not, Francesca leapt ahead as she got out of bed and shook grief off like a bad cold.

Sloane had watched Francesca move, both trapped in themselves. Motionless in the corner, she'd stayed glued to the only place in the room where she could see the entire apartment. Molly had come back to check on her. In silence, she had roamed through and into the movers as they packed Sloane into pieces of cardboard and tape.

The emptier the room had become, the emptier Sloane felt.

Francesca would live in a home Sloane hadn't. The Gray had been thick in her lungs.

A shaky voice grounded her back onto the plane she'd body-melded on. The elderly woman who sat beside Francesca said, "Beautiful sky outside, isn't it?" to no one in particular. Her voice lit up in surprise when waterworks followed the benign comment. "What's wrong dear?"

Sloane left the wealthy man's body and entered the finally sleeping man on the other side of Francesca. Only using sleeping people meant less stretching and no bathroom breaks. Dreams could be a problem, such as the horsey rides and mud pies the wealthy man had in mind, but she was working on blocking those out.

Though she'd have to watch out of the corner of her eye, Sloane was front row to Francesca's conversation.

She knew listening was wrong, but she didn't care.

Wrinkled hands reached for Francesca's smooth tan ones.

"It's just that..." Pain caressed Francesca's strong, yet delicate features. She was a beautiful crier. "Sloane..." Francesca stared straight ahead after a deep breath. The Gray spun. Did Francesca feel her? "She died," Francesca continued and turned a little to face the woman. "It's been one year and nine days." The plastic cup she'd been holding crinkled.

'Oh, my love. Don't keep track of the days,' Sloane wanted to say.

"I just packed up everything from our house to move to one my mother is buying me in Italy." She chuckled a little. "I'm still reeling that she's buying me a house. That's how much she wanted me there. In truth, there is nothing left for me in San Francisco–that's where we lived, San Francisco. We hated it almost as much as we loved it, but nowhere else felt like home."

"Would you like to tell me about her?" The woman's kind

lined face held sincerity. She had to be someone's grandmother. If not, she ought to be.

Francesca nodded. "If you truly don't mind. I don't want to interrupt what you were doing."

She clicked the grey tray back up into its rightful position and smiled encouragingly. "I think my crossword puzzles will keep. So, how long were you together?"

She turned a little. "Six beautiful years. It was our anniversary when... That fucking truck driver." She spat. "He was drunk. It's the oldest story in the book. One swerve, and everything's changed forever. The thing was, I wasn't going very fast, but the tree didn't move, did it? She flew through the window like a rag doll. My perfect Sloane, buckled in, flew from the shattered windshield and onto a branch. After... she wasn't her." Even describing one of the most painful events of her life, Francesca still had a way with words.

Sloane supposed she should have guessed that it had been a branch that gutted her. To her, it was as if she were watching a film through a blurry lens. She couldn't stop shivering. Francesca was dealing with more than she knew. So why did she almost kiss Cecelia?

"She was a fiery red-head, shorter than me, which I love. She had so many tattoos I liked to recount them when she slept, tracing each one so I wouldn't forget a single one. She had one for every place she'd ever called home—not just cities either. She'd been homeless for a while because of a horrible mother, so she got a large wooden spool on her back, which represented the time she'd stayed in a construction site. One was a small wolf from her time in the woods. She'd seen a wolf there and thought, 'I could stay here with the wolves, and no one would miss me.' Hearing that one broke my heart. There are many more small images, and they all fit in a fish tank. That was for when she'd snuck into a dentist's office to steal toothpaste and floss. She had a pill bottle with states for pills. Each one was home in its own right, too. She doesn't–didn't–tell them as sad stories. Just stories. And she had so many! By the time she met me, she'd been so many people. I've had just the one life, while she... she had twelve?"

Thirteen, when you include the most important one.

"Sloane was magic in a woman. I am lucky to have had her for as long as I did. But it's not fair that I'm here, and she's not. She should be the one here, not me. Once... oh, I'm going on. I'm sorry." Lifting herself up, she adjusted herself in the under-stuffed blue seat.

The woman shook her head; soft lilac waves moved ever-so-slightly. "No, dear. I'm enjoying hearing about her. Besides, you must keep those lost alive through stories. So, you were saying?"

Francesca's face brightened.

Sloane felt a tugging sensation in her chest, an invisible hand grabbing at her. Before she had a chance to push away from it, the sleeping man she'd inhabited expelled her.

"What the–" Sloane began.

"Once, we went to the beach in March. The water was frigid, but she desperately wanted to recreate the scene from The Note-book. She's not one for romance films, mind you. That one got to her, though. But it got my friend's stoic dad too."

Molly slipped out of her body and waved her arms at a flus-tered Sloane. "Calm down. You aren't ready to keep one for a long time yet. It's something you have to work on."

"–good cry after we watched it."

"Is Gregory your husband?" Francesca pointed to her large diamond and the two diamond crusted bands flanking it.

"You mean this will happen every time?" Sloane asked, still trying to listen to the conversation beside her.

The woman's voice held a tinge of sadness. "–haven't been

able to visit him in two months–troubles with my visa. Now, I can go be closer to him."

"Only for a little while. Each time gets easier. You can try again," Molly said.

"–two live?"

Sloane stopped and turned towards the women. She'd lost track of the conversation.

Deep set blue eyes seemed to darken, as she said, "His ashes are in a small Catholic church outside of Florence. I'm moving as close as I can." Before Francesca could reply, the woman said, "So you two were at the beach with cold water."

Never one to push, she marched forward. Her voice held less joy as she finished the story. "We both got bathing suits like Allie–"

"Maybe I'll wait. Just hover over here by Francesca." Sloane regretted not doing so the entire time.

"–the size of baseballs. We ran through the water screaming, 'If you're a bird, I'm a bird.' She'd been so happy; I almost forgot how miserable I was. She told me once that every time she went somewhere, she wanted to make a memory. She never just wanted to watch a movie or walk through a craft fair; she wanted to have breakfast at midnight after the movie to talk about it with a jukebox playing in the background and pancakes in her face. We'd buy something useless at the craft fair so we had to find a way to use it or a place to put it. Then, we'd have made a memory. I'm sure it's because of her childhood."

Got it in one.

Francesca's freckles had the uneven coloring they did when she held back tears. "I'm just glad she wanted to make all of those memories with me. It made every occasion with her special."

It really did.

Covering the woman's hand with hers, she asked, "Would you like to tell me about Gregory?"

"After I take a nap, dear. I'm getting a little tired." She slipped her hand from underneath Francesca's and patted it again. "I'm glad you told me about Sloane. Maybe you could tell me more later."

"That sounds fine. By the way, I never got your name."

"Just call me Rosa." From under her seat, she pulled a plaid blanket.

"I'm Francesca. It's nice to meet you, Rosa. Oh, before you head off to a nap, I just thought I'd tell you that I'm not moving far from Florence. If you're ever interested, we could meet for lunch and talk about anything or nothing. I only know a few people in Italy as it is."

"That sounds lovely, dear. Simply–"

Molly's voice jackhammered over the sweet moment. "Can we take our leave now? At least you know she still loves you."

25

FRANCESCA

Francesca smiled a little as she drove towards Mama's villa. For one beautiful moment, a fleeting image of Sloane's red hair in a massive frizzy bun and her only-for-my-love smile had Francesca buzzing. She must be overly excited. Finally, they'd moved to Italy. Their stuff would arrive in a few days, and they'd have picked out a place by then. It took a few blinks–almost a blissful three-seconds–before the realization that had her clenching her chest every morning hit her.

The sky dimmed, and her thoughts turned to Sloane's inside out body and leaf covered hair. Sloane was dead, and she was moving to Italy alone. Francesca blamed the breeze for her momentary, wistful forgetfulness. Turning on the air conditioning gave her some control.

The next leg of the drive was sluggish. Even the car seemed to creep a bit, use more gas, whine at her as she encouraged it with foul language to help her make it to a bed quicker.

When the silhouette of Mama's villa came into view, Francesca's eyes burned. The word 'mistake' stuck in her brain like a dart on a board. Her drive up the hill happened in an instance, and then she was parking in the driveway.

What kind of driving was that called? The scary kind? She had barely hugged Mama before strolling into the kitchen for a large glass of wine. Mama let Francesca take the reins of the afternoon.

Francesca seized that opportunity to drink three more glasses of some weak flowery white and conk out on top of freshly laundered sheets with her shoes still on.

DEJA VU.

Francesca awoke to the smell of cinnamon rolls, surrounded by fluffy white cotton. With sore eyes and a swollen face, she felt as though she were standing still. Any progress made had backslid when she'd gone home to San Francisco.

She admonished herself immediately. Grief was a process. Her progress in that process was going in the wrong direction. She'd take life slower this time.

Her problem? She hadn't been around other people for so long she was swept up in the normality of it all. Francesca decided she'd treat it as if the last three weeks had been a dream and start from the beginning.

When Mama padded into her room with a plate full of pastry and icing, Francesca knew she had to pick out a place and move sooner than later. She may have decided against the villa, but she couldn't live with Mama. Not cooking was nice, but it was time for her to work life out for herself. This time, she wouldn't be fully alone.

"Thought you might want something sweet before breakfast. You've been sleeping for a day and a half. I knew you'd need a pick-me-up if you were going to get out of bed."

"This isn't breakfast?"

Mama shook her head as she hopped up onto the foot of the

bed. It barely shifted. "We are meeting Alma in an hour. You'll be meeting your realtor for some house hunting today! I know you probably don't feel up to it, but I thought—"

"No, it's great. Thank you. Anyone else going to be there?" Francesca tried to casually ask as she stuffed a large chunk of a roll into her cheek. Icing dripped onto her chin. After she'd licked it off, she wanted to wipe her sticky hands off, but Mama had forgotten a napkin, and the bathroom was a few steps too far away for her liking, so her plane-stenched jeans would have to do.

"No, Essie. I wouldn't bring her on your first day back. You and Cecelia will talk, or not, in your own time. Alma and I agree on that."

"You talked about us?" Francesca flared and squeezed the nearest pillow so tightly she wondered if it would ever poof back up.

Mama threw her hands up. "Calm down. Alma mentioned that Cecelia was upset. I said Francesca too. We just agreed—we wouldn't meddle. It's very out of our nature, you know. But given the circumstances, we are trying. So don't charge at me. Or her, for that matter. We are doing our best here. It's odd for us. Now, do you want a caffè or no?"

"I'll take wine. My head's pounding and my knee is a little swollen from the plane and drive here." Francesca's small-framed mother hopped down to leave. "Mama? Thank you. It means a lot that you aren't getting involved. I do know it's hard for you. I love you."

Pushing undone, unruly hair out of the way, Mama turned to Francesca. "I love you too, Essie. Now, grab a shower. The wine will be here for you when you're done."

～

THE BELL above the entrance *tinked.* Alma didn't turn; she was laughing with, presumably, the server. He wore a too-small black waist apron.

"Ah, here they are! And early, still." She tapped her over-sized, yet simple leather-banded watch. "I should know by now; Maria's never late. And Francesca! It's so good to see you again." Alma stood to kiss them on both of their cheeks. "Karl, these are the Nuccio women. Beautiful, no? This is Karl, a friend of a friend. He's a transplant like you Francesca." Alma waved her arms as if he was a 'Brand New Car!' on a game show.

"Nice to meet you." Francesca flashed him a hopefully sincere smile.

Karl scratched at his crooked and flat nose. "You as well, pardon my Italian. I'm fluent, not yet. One of the sentences know I the best." He was charming. German, maybe. With so many accents around and names that could come from anywhere, Francesca couldn't tell; it felt rude to ask.

"You're doing great so far, Karl." Francesca kept her eyes on the menu she wasn't reading.

Window seats were Francesca's favorite, and Alma had procured a scuffed white metal table with odd chair choices near the open door. However, Karl was too tall for so early in the morning; looking at his face caused Francesca to stare directly into the sun.

"Thank you. I'll take order?" He pulled a pencil from behind his ear and held onto his pad of paper for dear life.

"Let's give them a minute to look at the menu," Alma spoke sweetly.

"Of course." As Karl left, Francesca began to squint. His kinky dark brown hair had blocked out more rays than she thought.

A few landscape photographs hung on the white walls, and a gargoyle angel statue sat on the counter by the cash register.

Mismatched hard chairs crowded tables of all materials. It felt as if they were in a room of garage sale finds.

"So Francesca, I hear you're looking for a home. That's so exciting! Your Mama and I thought for sure you'd like the villas. Since those weren't right, we'll need more to go on." Alma shifted in her wooden spindle-backed chair.

"Of course. When's the realtor showing up?"

They laughed, their eyes flicked back and forth to each other, and a wicked smile broke across their faces.

Alma spoke first. "We're already here."

Francesca groaned and not from the dull ache the polypropylene math class-style chair caused. "If it was you two who were going to help me, why didn't you just say so?"

"Well, I thought it would be better–oh, wait! Is that Vito?" Mama stopped short and pointed at a couple on the sidewalk.

Alma shouted his name as he pushed the glass door open for the woman in a blue striped dress. A pink-faced Vito stopped, while she shuffled to the table furthest from the window; she did not introduce herself.

"Good morning, ladies. You all look beautiful. Are you having a nice breakfast?"

Mama smiled and nodded. "It's going well. Who's that with you? I thought you were–"

"She's a friend from college. She's only in town for a week, so we are out to breakfast." Beady brown eyes shifted around the room, while sweat began to dot Vito's round face.

"Ah, I see. Well, you say hi to Silvia, wouldn't you?" Alma said pointedly.

Mama's teeth showed. "Yes. Tell her it's been a while and to call us. We'd love to have dinner sometime."

He bolted away with a nod; they chose not to stay for breakfast.

"I can't believe he'd parade someone around like that. We all know they are having problems, but that's distasteful." Mama said before the door had shut. Francesca saw stripes swirl as the woman whipped around to have a listen two-seconds too late.

"Mama," Francesca refocused. "My house?"

She couldn't get swept up in a stranger's spousal drama. Her own guilt ulcer had already made a home in her stomach the moment Alma hugged her.

"Does it always have to be about you?" Mama smacked her head with her letter—in a new envelope. "Just tell us what you're looking for." It was as if Francesca had been holding them up. "Alma and I know everyone—Montepulciano is a small place—and we're going to find you the perfect place."

Francesca worried the next few hours would end in screams.

Trying to be open-minded, she said, "I want some place with emotion behind it; a place with a story to share. I got swept up in the idea of a large villa and fancy vineyard, but I don't need those things. Honestly, I couldn't take care of those things. I want a smaller place and no yard. Show me the places most people think are too weird." 'Because Sloane would be happier somewhere odd.'

"Alright. Let's eat. Then, I have a few places in mind," Alma said.

Mama nodded. "Me too. Where were you thinking?"

They spoke in code: using names and street addresses. Francesca didn't become more curious or excited. Instead, it just stressed her out.

Karl ambled back to the table. "Having what are you?" Each time he was so close.

Francesca started intently at the menu as she ordered eggs and potatoes. Karl didn't notice her lack of eye contact; good. How could she have said he was too tall for her liking?

When the food arrived, Francesca ate the eggs in two bites.

They were tasteless. Whether that was the cook's fault or her depressed tastebuds didn't much matter.

"Ready to go, I see?" Mama teased.

"What can I say? You were talking about some interesting sounding places, and I'm excited," laughed The Lying Liar from Liarsville. Part of her wanted to drop the fork that was mechanically stabbing potatoes and shoving them into her fake mouth and run to the airport.

Alma smiled and waved Karl to them, handing him her card before anyone else could offer money. "I'm surprised you heard us over your fast chewing." Playful eyes sparkled.

"Are you sure you don't want to split the check?"

Francesca would be getting her apartment's hefty deposit back any day, so she could afford a few breakfasts before her bank reached a dangerously low number.

"Yes, Maria got it last time."

"It's what we do," Mama said. "Once you have a nice job and settle in, maybe you can contribute. For now, put your money in a savings account. We can take care of you for a few months."

Alma nodded. "We only just stopped paying for Tony at places because the restaurant we bought him is making money."

"You both bought it?" Francesca asked, floored.

When had she and Alma become thick as thieves? Mama had talked about her, sure, but they had to trust each other a great deal to put that kind of money in one investment.

Alma popped a bite of toast into her mouth and nodded. "Strong women stick together," she said as she swallowed. "We've got three other women who pitch in sometimes. We all help the kids until they are good and making their way. It's not common everywhere, and it's not city-wide to be sure, but we have a small community. It's a good way to keep the wealth you have: invest it in your children. In my case, my money comes from the family winery and my ex-husband. What else would I spend it all on if not my children?"

"That's why, Essie, I bought the vineyard. Hopefully, the grapes will grow in this year now that I've got a good gardener." Mama took a sip of her water. "It will be a nice source of income in addition to the family money, alimony, and survivor's benefits."

"Survivor's what?"

Mama choked on air. "Nothing, I misspoke."

"Mama," Francesca warned.

Alma announced her need for a restroom–an excellent choice.

"It's from a friend from long ago," Mama said cryptically before Alma had taken two steps.

"No, not enough. People don't get survivor's benefits for being a friend. I lost Sloane, and no one's sending me money. We were much more than friends. So, what's going on?"

Mama pulled out the letter, and Francesca reared up. "Don't you dare smack me now! I asked you a question."

"And I'm answering it." Mama became so small, so little; Francesca's shoulders fell.

Karl came up to ask if they needed anything, as Alma had signed the check already.

"Thanks, we're okay. Just chatting a bit, then we'll be out of your hair."

He smiled. "No rush! Mama Loreti tips enough me for you to all day stay if you want."

"Of course she does." Francesca loved that.

A new world she entered; Mama never let her money show. They saved a lot, spent on what they needed and enough to have some wants–never all. Francesca never went without but had never been spoiled. This overt display of wealth was foreign to her.

"So, Mama. You were saying?"

"Just read the letter." Her eyes brimmed. "And I'm not crying for what you're about to read. I'm crying because Sloane kept her promise to me."

"Sloane? What does Sloane have to do with any of this? And wait, you called her Sloane."

"Read the letter; then I'll explain everything."

"Dear Mrs. Temple,"

Francesca stopped reading. "Mrs. Temple? Who's Mrs. Temple?"

"Do you want me to tell you, or..."

"No, no. I can read it."

Francesca swatted Mama with the letter. And though Francesca had wanted to do such many times as a child, it held no satisfaction. "Oh, Mama," she said after a second. "Oh, Mama!"

Francesca's face became damp. Mama let a tear drop but held back the rest.

Alma peeked her head out from the bathroom but stayed put when she saw the tears.

"I've had a complicated life, Essie. I loved a man—a soldier—named George Temple. It was the kind of love you only have once. I saw that love in you and Susan; I'm sorry, I saw that in you and *Sloane*."

Francesca bit the inside of her cheek.

"George and I married very young, 16. A few months after we were married, he was called to fight in the Vietnam War. It was nearly over, so we both figured it wouldn't be that bad. Childish thoughts; foolish thoughts. 'That bad'? It was a war." She shook her head and sighed. "The first letter I received said he was missing in action. I kept that one too, but it's been ripped up and taped back together; I've tucked it away."

Francesca thought to hold Mama's hand, but she was fidgeting with her clean napkin.

"He was presumed dead after seven years. That letter is in a small plastic bag, shredded into bits. This letter, however, this letter came when you were three-years-old. George's body had been found. He'd been a prisoner of war for two years."

Francesca gasped and reached for Mama's hand.

Mama let her hold it. "It was the catalyst for me divorcing your father, to be honest. He was no George; I'm sorry to say. But you were the best thing that had ever happened to me, so I changed our last name back to my great-grandfather's, and we moved to New Mexico."

Francesca was dumbfounded. A massive chunk of her mother's life just clicked together like a puzzle.

"I told Sloane about this six months before the accident. We were a bit tipsy on too many martinis or glasses of wine, who can remember those kinds of things? I told her what I just told you; then I asked her to let me tell you in my own time. It was a big ask, to hold a secret like this. But she did. And that touched my heart more than she could imagine. Sometimes I'd swear she was here. In some ways, I want her to be, but in others, I hope she's where she should be. Either way, I hope she knows how proud I am of her, and proud that she was my daughter-in-law. You may have never married, but in my eyes, it was all but done."

Shocked, Francesca coughed out, "Mine too."

A lump sat in her throat. She had no idea Mama had felt any of that; she hadn't expressed it when Sloane had been alive. Sloane had assured Francesca that Mama liked her, despite Francesca's fears.

As usual, Sloane had been right.

If only she had been able to tell her how she had known.

"I'm sorry I've kept this from you. In some ways it means nothing, in others, it's everything. I just haven't been able to tell you."

"I'm glad you told me. There are no words for how sorry I am that you lost your love. I see now why you understood so much when I first got here. I love you, Mama. You can tell me anything. I hate that you've been holding this in for so long. Did you tell my bio-dad?"

"I did. It was a hard conversation that brought up a lot of emotions, but we weren't happy before that." She paled a little. "Oh! You didn't need to know that; he's still your dad."

"It's okay, Mama. I'm glad I never blamed myself, though," Francesca joked, attempting to bring her mother back from her dark place. Francesca frequented that place.

Mama slid the letter back into its new envelope and playfully smacked Francesca on the hand. "Thank you. It's nice to have this out in the open."

"No more secrets? And no more smacking me with letters?"

"No more secrets," Mama agreed. "As for the letter... well, it has come in handy. I think I'll keep it around."

They stood and hugged.

Francesca's tailbone throbbed from the angle of the seat—meant to keep you alert and uncomfortable. Creases on her mother's face softened; her chair looked worse than Francesca's.

Alma appeared, clearly pleased they'd finished. "Thought I'd live in the bathroom. You two all set to visit some potential homes?"

"Ready." Mama nodded, impressed by her lack of pressing. She grabbed her purse—letter zipped up tight and glanced at Francesca.

Filled with genuine optimism, Francesca agreed. "Yes, I think I am."

The three stepped out into the warmth, and Mama seemed lighter. "Alright, Alma, what do you think? Glass Staircase first?"

"Oh yes," Alma said, as she swept her hair into an elegant bun. She used two bobby pins to hold it together. "I think that place is great. It can get a bit warm, but there are a fair number of windows, all made by the owner, which help it a lot. Let's take my car."

~

THROUGH THE WINDOW, Francesca watched a lamp-worker in a black apron spin a ball of molten glass into a crystal unicorn.

Treasures from the compact glass blowing studio glittered, and rainbows danced on the stones of the street.

Mama gently guided Francesca towards the side of the shop. "Over here."

Francesca's shoulders hunched in disappointment; she wished they could stay to watch longer. Still, she moved towards a small alleyway. Odors of sweat, beeswax, and fire accosted her when she opened the door that led to the loft above the Glass Staircase. She breathed through her nose; she couldn't imagine tasting the smell. Visitors and tour guides' chatter fell away as the door clicked behind them. The blissful silence nearly made up for the smell.

Alma jogged in front of her to unlock the door and open a window. She turned to Francesca. "It's not a huge space, but it's unique."

"It could be something." Mama echoed.

Paint half of the cement wall, hang a few pictures from the plaster ones, and they were right. It would be bright and strange.

The hum of the kindling furnace below her would be the soundtrack to her life, just as the dripping water had been in San Francisco. Built-in cabinets wrapped around a modest kitchen. With a coat of white and turquoise with a few knobs here and there...

Odd twists of pulled glass with naked bulbs hanging from them decorated the vaulted, water splotched ceiling. Sloane would have swooned. Francesca smiled despite herself, just thinking of Sloane nestled by the open window reading a book.

The bathroom was adorable. Having a claw foot tub would have had Sloane salivating, as she had always wanted to have a long soak with a shower cap in an old bathtub. Francesca never understood the appeal.

"So?" Mama asked.

There went Francesca's off-the-rails train of thought; it was for the best.

"I like it. The heat isn't great, though." She would have to have quite a few fans in the small home. With only one-half wall separating the bedroom from the main room, it shouldn't be that hot–even in the summer. Her potential soundtrack may be the deal-breaker. "It's definitely a contender. I see the potential, but I still want to see what else there is."

Alma and Mama looked at each other. Both were a little dewy but smiling. "I'm glad we're on the right track," Alma said. "How about we go to The Floral Palace next?"

"Sure. That's a darling name. Let me guess; it's by a florist?"

They both nodded.

"Yes. It used to be called Pilla's Florist, but at some point she decided she didn't want a nickname any longer or maybe she didn't like it? She's fickle. So she went with what the tourists would flock to the most." Alma had her head tilted down as she shook it and laughed. "She *has* had more business since. She knows her audience. The home next to her shop is for sale. Pilla–I mean Patrizia–bought it to expand, but ended up wanting a second location instead. Now she wants to sell her place and focus her attention on that. It's a great price. Not that you should concern yourself with that, Francesca. We want you to be happy, of course!"

Alma drove them a few miles down the road to a small alcove of stores. A fruit stand sat beside a grocery shop. Two clothing stores were on either side of The Floral Palace's duplex. Small homes were peppered in between and on top of them.

"Would I have someone living above me?" Francesca asked. She didn't want to have an apartment-like home.

Searching for a parking spot seemed to take all of Alma's mental energy. Francesca wasn't sure she'd even heard the question.

"No. You'll have both floors, but hold your horses," Mama said, using one of Francesca's favorite phrases from when she was a little girl.

"You got it, Mama."

Parking would undoubtedly be a nightmare when Francesca's car arrived. "Are there no spots for tenants?"

"Sadly, no."

They may as well turn around and go. Unless the place was perfect, Francesca couldn't imagine herself fighting with shoppers to get into her own home.

She'd take a look because they were already there.

Almost five minutes of roaming two parking lots finally yielded a skinny spot that took five attempts to fit in without breaking a mirror. Getting out of the car was a joke.

Good thing they were all small. Mama could fit almost anywhere.

"Finally," Alma said once they were on the sidewalk. "This way."

Francesca wanted to be a petulant child, and beg the question, 'Why would you bring me here? This is horrible.' Then, the familiar Italian scents hit her nose, and she knew.

Fresh bread sat in the window of the grocery store, and The

Floral Palace's shop doors were open, sharing fresh cut flowers with the passersby. Sloane's thoughts popped into her head again. She'd smell the pesticides and be turned off. The parking would have been a deal-breaker, as they said if they ever moved, they'd have to have a parking spot. Street parking had been more than a little irritating.

"You have a face," Mama announced. "I see your brain working. You've already decided against this place, haven't you?"

Francesca scrunched her mouth to the side.

"Ah," Alma said. "Should we head back now?"

"No, no! Let's see it. Can't hurt, right?" Francesca felt awful. She used to be a good poker player. "It's the parking. But I adjusted in San Francisco. So maybe it wouldn't be that bad if the place is great."

"That's the spirit!" Alma's sweaty face brightened. They had a decent walk from the car to the duplex.

Mama knew Francesca was full of it. The likelihood she'd change her mind had always been slim. Sloane would have known that too. Stomach and heart doing a flip, Francesca's brain couldn't get Sloane's face out of her mind. She shouldn't be house shopping without her. No tears. Francesca would not let herself cry–not then. Sloane would be as present as she could be in her new place, and that's all Francesca could do.

"Maybe we should head to the next place," Alma suggested after they did the quickest tour possible.

The Miami retirement home vibe stunted even Mama's imagination. The walls were pastel green and had a palm tree wallpaper, the furniture, all white wicker; Francesca couldn't have seen beyond that, even if the parking had been perfect.

"Giorgia owns a used bookstore and the floor above it which she converted into a loft. The stairs have become a problem, so she's selling the loft. It needs some work, but more cosmetic than anything." A sly smile slid onto Francesca's face as mixed emotions rolled over her. "I know," Mama said. "We should have shown it to you first. I wanted to make sure you saw something else before you went with the familiar."

"I wasn't going to say anything." Just *think* it. "I'm just excited to see it."

"It's the closest to me too," Mama added quietly, and her eyes sparkled.

"That's a bonus then, isn't it?"

Alma sighed. "She's going to go with that one no matter what, isn't she? You were right all along." Her voice held amusement despite how harried she seemed.

"I loved the first place too. Already picked out paint colors. This place will have to impress the hell out of me to top it."

A SILENT TEAR trickled down her face as the smell of old books overwhelmed her. Flowers, fresh bread, leather, and charred paper vanished.

"Well, that's it then. She's sold, and we haven't even been inside." Alma studied Francesca.

Embarrassed, Francesca wished her emotions away.

Mama didn't whisper when she told Alma, "It was a year less than two weeks ago."

Alma paused as if formulating the perfect sentence. "From what I've heard, she was a beautiful soul." Her voice made each word somewhere between a sigh and a cry.

Francesca–too choked up to reply–stepped into Alma's open arms.

Mama held Francesca's hand as they stepped on creaky, knotted wooden floors through the rows and rows of books in mahogany bookshelves. When they reached the back of the store, there was a small door. 'Not Yours,' it read. Too perfect.

Of course Mama had been worried she wouldn't want to see anything else.

One of the steps wobbled as they walked up to Giorgia's home. "That will have to be fixed," Francesca said aloud.

"As I said, a project. Oh, I nearly forgot to hand you the key. I thought you might want to do the unlocking."

A real skeleton key appeared from Mama's purse.

"Are you serious? It's kind of heavy; is it real?" A giddiness built up in her; she'd nearly forgotten how it felt. Legs bouncing in anticipation, Francesca couldn't unlock the door quick enough.

The key slid in the iron lock and clicked twice as she turned it. When Francesca pushed the heavy door, the familiar smell of old, dust, and perfume escaped into the hallway. Her cheeks hurt as she coughed and smiled.

"It's bigger than it seems," Mama offered.

A purple and cream fleur de leis wallpaper covered every wall, and the floors seemed to be original hardwood. The living room alone was larger than Francesca and Sloane's apartment in San Francisco; the bedroom was about the same size. A clawfoot tub sat in a decent sized bathroom that screamed for new flooring and a new sink. The cabinets, flooring, and appliances in the kitchen would have to be removed too, but it was a nice size and had a lot of light. The building not being attached to another made for great visibility.

Windows flooded the house with light, and none were alike. Some were small circles as though they'd been stolen from a submarine. Others were large squares able to open so wide Francesca worried her arms weren't long enough to close them again; she found a pulley before a real panic set in. Two windows looked as if they'd been plucked from a Catholic church; colored sunlight bounced onto the floors. She opened all of them—just to see.

Fresh air wafted in, as if she were in the country, while the vents let the book scent trickle up. Noise from people milling below was muffled despite the eleven open windows. She only heard the occasional angry or impatient driver honking and slamming on their brakes. That boded well for sleep,

Spinning around in the living room, Francesca saw her belongings there. Sloane's library would go along the walls. Her bedroom would have a bookshelf or two, as well. Paint colors were coming to her, but she'd have to strip the walls to see the light on bare walls before she decided. The place was perfect. Sloane would love it here.

Francesca's hand clutched the key so hard it left an imprint inside of her hand pressed against her heart. She wandered to the front door where Alma and Mama stood. They were quietly chatting about how much it would cost and how long it would take to fix the place up.

"And what have you come up with?" Francesca pushed back her slowly frizzing dark hair. Maybe she should cut it; to the middle of her back seemed too long.

"What?" Mama asked.

"How much would it cost? Is it too expensive?"

Alma's eyes twinkled almost as much as Mama's. "Of course not."

"Our children's happiness is worth everything to us, Essie. And the way you're all curled up, the way you are when something is like magic to you, says this is the one. Am I wrong?"

"You're not. It's exactly what I need. Sloane breathes here with me, but I don't think I'll cry every day. Does that make sense?"

Alma answered while Mama's eyes welled. She must have been thinking about her George. "Yes, yes, it does. I, too, lost someone. It was so long ago, but he'll live with me always. If ever I stop feeling his presence..." She broke off. Vulnerability painted Alma's face. Of course, when she thought about it, she knew everyone had depths and pain they held close.

Francesca grabbed both her mother and Alma and squeezed them tight. The three had shared a moment. It would take them all a moment to shake out of it. By the time they made it to the front door of the shop, they were all back to being the women who stomped down the streets with their head held high, no insecurities in sight.

"I'll call Lisa while we grab lunch. When we get home, we can start designing your dream home."

Mama was in such a good mood, she practically skipped.

Francesca was going to live in Italy, only ten minutes away from her. Francesca would be okay. At some point.

26

SLOANE

Out of the open arched bedroom window, Francesca whispered, "I haven't talked to you in a while. But I wanted to tell you that I love you. I think of you every day and miss you more than words. If you can hear me, then you've probably seen what a mess I am. I know it may look like I'm moving on, but I'm just moving. If I stop, I may be the person I was right after the accident. I can't be her again."

She pushed at her lower eyelids, and Sloane reached for her.

"I'm almost out of your perfume. I thought maybe it had been you who'd opened it before. I'm thinking about ordering a new one to sit in with your books. Is that weird?"

Sloane shook her head. "No, that's why I sprayed it for you," she replied despite it going unheard by Francesca.

Only Molly could have heard her then.

Shaking the wistfulness away, Francesca slammed the old window closed. Fluffing her hair as she often did before entering a new room seemed to give her the confidence needed to walk back into the living room. Mama Nuccio and Cecelia's mother were talking about money. A few words were foreign to Sloane; that annoyed her.

"And what have you come up with?" Francesca put her hand on her hip.

Sloane roamed the house more thoroughly as the women discussed. Francesca was going to buy the house, what else did she need to know?

27

FRANCESCA

Time moved so quickly over the week. In the two days it took for her furniture and car to make their way to her, Francesca worked on her new home, became acquainted with the nearby shops, and befriended Giorgia Orbel–her new neighbor/seller of her home. Often, Francesca had to stop and remind herself she wasn't dreaming. Italian may be her new permanent language as Italy may be her new permanent home. Too surreal.

A demolition and renovation would have been a project Sloane wanted to do. Without her, Francesca had no real desire to dig deep, get dirty and sweaty. Help would be lacking, after all. She pictured her mother ripping down wallpaper. On a ladder, Mama would pick at one small spot with a spackling tool and mumble about how it would have been easier to hire someone. God only knew what would happen if she hurt herself. No, Francesca couldn't see anyone but contractors doing the job.

Most of her work involved pointing and saying, "That one." Or shaking her head and telling them, "Absolutely not." She felt so lazy. Francesca had always imagined herself being more active in designing her first home–with Sloane.

On one of the hottest days of the year, she got a call from the contractors. Her nearly renovated home was ready to be inhabited. A few to-dos still loomed, but she could move in and decorate.

Mama insisted on being there when she walked in for the first time, of course. "Well?" She asked as they opened the door.

"It smells horrible." Francesca thought to pull her hair out of its ponytail holder to cover her nose. Her tank top wouldn't be of any help.

"That's paint, Essie. Your old book smell will come back in no time. The bookstore can't help itself." Mama chuckled. She was already walking to the largest window in the living room; Francesca could only imagine her smile.

"When the smell is gone, I'll come back."

"You can see some of it now!" Mama huffed so dramatically her curls bounced around her shoulders. "Why can't you just get past the smell and look around? It's exactly what you wanted. It's perfect."

Francesca deflated. "I don't want the magic to be gone. Part of it was the smell, I'm sure of it."

"I know, darling. But that will come back in time. It will also smell like you and what you do, or cook. Just come see it."

"You're right. It's just been–"

"A long week to say the least. Yes, I know."

Mama pushed Francesca into the living room. The foyer still had a small strip of wallpaper; in the end, Francesca couldn't bear to see it all go. She'd put a cute chair there with a few boxes of shoes. Light grey paint covered the living room walls. Years of neglect had left the baseboard trim yellowed.

After the painters came through, it had become a fresh, nearly too-bright white once again. Each window was cleaned and resealed. They had added a bench under the picture window in the living room, and a patio now bumped out from her bedroom.

"It's... it's..."

They'd painted her future sanctuary cream with a splash of peach towards the top of the walls. It looked hastily painted, just as she requested–a look Sloane had always wanted. Francesca could smile more and mourn less when Sloane's designs surrounded her.

"Go step out onto the patio. I think you'll love the view."

"It's huge!" Francesca exclaimed as she pushed the French doors outward.

Wrought iron bars in a long s-shape framed the new patio. A table and two chairs sat on top of the floor made of rounded stone pieces. Francesca had asked for a personal French bistro in the middle of Italy; they'd delivered.

Mama linked arms with Francesca. "So you like it?"

"Like it? I love it! It's exactly what I wanted."

Francesca inhaled her new homey scents, ignoring the paint stench behind them.

"And the view...?"

"Is that what I think it is?"

"Yes! We almost put the patio from the kitchen, so you could have people wander onto it. But we figured it was better to have this view and keep it to yourself." Mama's eyes found her lilac ballet flats to be fascinating as she added, "I hope we did the right thing."

"Mama, you got it right. You should put a large flag in your yard whenever you want me to come over. I bet I could see it."

"You know, I hadn't thought of that. Except that I did; it's got a big rainbow on it. I thought you'd appreciate that."

Suppressing a teenage-sound, Francesca reminded her mother, "I told you, everything doesn't have to have a rainbow on it." Mama's face fell a little. This project had her overly emotional. "But I'm glad it does because I'll know it was picked out just for me."

"I could return it."

"No, please don't. I mean it; I'm glad you picked it out for me. Thank you, Mama. Thank you for all of this! It's so perfect. I'll be indebted to you for forever. Wait, that's what this was, wasn't it? A way to make sure I'll live here forever?" Francesca laughed loudly.

Mama's eyes welled. "I love you."

"I love you too."

"I'm so happy you're here and even happier that you're smiling."

TONY AND A MAN Francesca had not met carried Sloane's precious bookcases through the store and up the stairs. She felt the need to shout a warning to be careful.

"Where's this one going, Frannie?" the new man asked, as they rested it on the floor, awaiting instructions.

"Don't call me that," Francesca snapped. The words flew out of her mouth like a dove from a top hat. Part of her wanted to take them back, but she decided against it. "Just keep lining the living room walls with the tallest bookshelves. You'll see. When you're done put the two shorter ones in the back left corner of my room, please. If there are any left, I'll look at the space and let you know."

"Why not Frannie?" Thick eyebrows shot up in what seemed like a genuine curiosity rather than irritation or amusement.

"It sounds like a feminine product."

Alma chuckled ruefully from the floor beside them. Francesca looked over her shoulder and saw with pleasure the rug Sloane had bought in Nevada was in the middle of her living room. Mama's laugh–loud, but quickly stifled–came from Francesca's bedroom.

The man who still hadn't introduced himself seemed unfazed. "I had an Aunt Frannie."

"Oh." Francesca's face warmed. "No offense."

"Everyone has their own way." What an odd phrase for a mid-twenty-something to use. But he was right. "Fine, no Frannie. I'll think of something else as we bring up these wooden beasts." He winked. "When's lunch?"

"It's 9 am, and you just got here twenty minutes ago," Tony replied quicker than Francesca. "Did you not have breakfast?"

"I did, but I already worked it off. Alright you, we should get back to it." He slapped Tony on the shoulder. "We've got a lot of carrying ahead of us before lunch, whenever it is."

Alma tugged at the silk scarf holding her hair up and chuckled as she opened another box of clothes. "Just like his father–my brother. When he finds a woman who can cook and thinks he's handsome, he'll end up married whether he likes her or not."

Mama had finished straightening out invisible creases from Francesca's perfectly made bed and was putting the expertly folded linens away. She and Alma had Francesca sitting on her hands a lot of the day as they insisted they could handle this and that. Before they'd arrived at 7:30 am, Francesca had fallen apart twice. Her face must have been puffy because their faces had shown sympathy the moment she opened the door.

"I think that's why this one's dad and I got married," she commented wryly.

Francesca perked up her ears as she dropped off boxes labeled 'Bathroom.'

"Why? Because you could cook?" Alma shouted across the house.

"And I thought he was good looking. I fed his stomach and

his ego. Is there much more a man needs? As for me, I guess I got swept up in the showered affection. Gifts are the way to my heart, it seems."

Though she laughed heartily, it rang hollow. It wasn't true. She'd been attempting to move on, and bio-dad happened to be nearby at the right time.

Cecelia sat cross-legged on the floor in the brand new pale green and cream kitchen complete with walnut cabinets. Francesca adored it, having personally designed it down to the pull knobs on the drawers.

At the moment, she couldn't go in. Since she'd come back to Italy, she and Cecelia hadn't spoken.

When Cecelia had knocked on the door around 8:30 am, Francesca's stomach flipped. She'd worn overalls, and her hair had been pulled back in a messy bun. All she'd said was, "Hey." Her beautiful thick accent had almost blurred the word into just a sound. They'd both stood there and shuffled their feet uncomfortably for thirty-seconds before their mothers had loudly torn open boxes to cut the tension. Cecelia had only blushed, while Francesca had been filled with too many emotions to know what to do with herself.

"Where to?" Cecelia had asked.

That'd put Francesca into unpacking mode. It had calmed her blood which seemed to be on the fritz–cold, hot; it couldn't decide.

"Kitchen. There are a ton of stacked boxes. I went through and wrote what should go where on each. They may not be perfect, so stick stuff wherever if you can't tell what I meant or if it was mislabeled. I just want the boxes out and my stuff somewhere. Organizing is next week's priority."

"Perfect." The sunlight that was pouring in from Francesca's myriad of windows had made Cecelia's eyes sparkle. It had made Francesca curse.

"Thanks for helping out." Francesca had retreated to her room to putz–another solid teenage moment. She'd almost moaned at her lack of maturity.

By seven, they were all moving so slowly, Francesca knew they should call it quits. The furniture was situated where it belonged, give or take a few inches. Stacked, broken down boxes leaned against the foyer door; they stood nearly as tall as Francesca.

Only eight unopened boxes remained by the bookcases: Sloane's books. No one was allowed to open those boxes but her.

When Cecelia had finished unpacking the kitchen, she'd tried.

"What are you doing?" Francesca's voice had come out harsh and ragged.

"Just moving to the living room. This box says, 'Third Shelf'. I figured I'd put it on one of the bookcases third shelf so I can toss out the box. I could come help you organize later this week if–"

"Don't open that box," she'd said sternly.

"Oh. Alright. I'm sorry, I just–"

"It doesn't matter."

Cecelia had stood and somewhat calmly decided to visit the closed bookstore below. Half an hour later, she'd come back with red eyes. She hadn't mentioned it again, and no one had made any more attempts to touch the boxes either.

"Dinner?" Tony asked when Francesca started to thank everyone and tell them she could take it from there.

"My treat!" How could Francesca have forgotten that?

"You haven't already called somewhere?" Tony's helper chastised in jest. "I guess I could–"

Cecelia swiveled to her brother. "Get on it, Tony."

Alma made a sound of agreement, and Mama added, "Have you been to the backyard patio? Giorgia said it's yours too. Sometimes she uses it during her lunch breaks, but otherwise."

Francesca felt giddy despite her worn out muscles. What'd made her so tired? What had she done today other than manage and grieve? Oh, right. "You forgot to mention the *second* patio!"

"Tony, go pick up some food. Augusto, would you grab us a few bottles of red? Cecelia, since you know where everything is at the moment, grab us some plates, utensils, and glasses. A pitcher too, if she has one. We have some celebrating to do."

Finally! She learned the man's name: Augusto. "I do–have a pitcher that is," Francesca said with amusement at Alma's perk-up and take-charge moment.

"Good. Then Augusto, grab a few glasses of water." She'd labeled him the fetching guy–poor thing.

"Francesca, Maria, and I will set up the patio, and see you all in half an hour." Alma stood and slipped off her headscarf. A layer of fuzz hovered over her usually smooth hair as if an electrical outlet zapped her. "Alright?"

As if they all just shouted "break," they dispersed.

Before Francesca knew it, the patio was transformed: leaves and brush swept away and lights woven into the vine-covered metal fence. They arranged a small patio set similar to Mama's and plopped into the cushions.

"We can go shopping for a longer table with comfortable chairs this week if you'd like?" Mama suggested. "Then you can be added in the host rotation." It wasn't a question as to if, more so when.

"Next week, please. Then the week after I'll be on rotation. I need a little more time."

"Of course, Essie."

"No rush, Francesca," Alma said, adjusting her top. "We've given Cecelia all the time in the world. And she's still not in the rotation, is she? She always says she's 'just now getting settled' and her job is 'very demanding.'"

As if to save the conversation from whatever direction it was headed in, the men strode up with the best distraction for any Italian: food and wine.

AFTER A LENGTHY DINNER, a little too much wine, and twenty minutes of goodbyes, the clock read 10:23 pm.

"I'm going to put up the flag before I go to bed. Keep an eye out tonight!" Mama said as she and Alma took turns hugging Francesca.

"Yes, Mama. I will, *if* you do it early. I'm exhausted."

"I love you, Essie."

"And I love you, Mama."

With another quick hug, she and Alma left, the men not far behind. Augusto insisted on downing any unfinished wine. "I'm not driving, eh?"

Cecelia hung back. As if they hadn't been around each other all day, she whispered, "Hey." That word.

"Oh, hey. Nice to see you again," Francesca joked. She began stacking the dishes up in the plastic recycling tub she'd brought to carry them back up.

"Let me help you."

Francesca paused. "No, it's okay. You've done plenty already. What's up?"

"Well, if we're cutting straight to it, I wanted to talk to you about Rome."

"Okay."

"Okay? We haven't spoken since, and then my mother tells me I am going to help you move into your new home. I didn't know you were moving here. Or that you'd left."

Since when did she have to tell Cecelia anything?

Cecelia must have read Francesca's thoughts. "I'm sorry." She grabbed the small metal trashcan and scraped dishes clean while she spoke. "This is going all wrong. I wanted to ask you if you ever wanted to see me again? I know this is a crazy thing you're going through. No, that's not true; I don't know–I can't even imagine. Mama told me a few weeks ago was a year. I'm so, so–" She'd put the plate down and touched Francesca's arm.

"Don't."

"I'm sorry. I don't know what the right thing is to do here. I don't think there is any."

For what? Francesca scraped the last dish Cecelia had stopped doing and put it in the tub. Two glasses and one take-out box stood in between Francesca going upstairs.

"I miss you. We were getting along really well."

"We were," Francesca agreed. To keep herself from looking at Cecelia, she tied the garbage bag closed and walked it to the dumpster on the other side of the building.

Cecelia trailed after her. "So, could we go for coffee some-time?" The sound of stupid skinny heels punctuated every word. "I'm not expecting anything. I know what almost happened in Rome may never happen again."

Metal hinges squeaked as Francesca tossed the trash in. "I'm j–I need a little time to settle in. But when I'm a little more settled, sure; we can get coffee." Before Cecelia could say anything else, Francesca added, "As friends."

"On your time," Cecelia added as they made their way back to the patio.

"That sounds good. Thank you for understanding."

"Why couldn't I open that box?"

Francesca winced at the question and the click of Cecelia's heels. "I don't want to talk about that."

"Was it something I can't see?"

Francesca picked up the tub of dishes and clenched it tightly. "Cecelia, they are my things. If I don't want you opening the box, you don't get to." It seemed harsh, but she still barely knew this woman. A week and a half of friendship doesn't warrant inquiries, despite the connection they may or may not have. "I'm sure there is plenty in your home that I can't see. We're barely friends. I hate to say it like that, but..."

"They were Sloane's things weren't they?"

After the last few weeks, hearing Cecelia say Sloane's name was a trigger. Eyes burning and body flashing, Francesca snapped. "Please go. I'll let you know when I'm up to talking."

"I hit a nerve. I'm sorry. I thought I ha–"

Francesca imagined Cecelia reaching out again, looking devastated by her faux pas. Instead of turning to confirm her thoughts, Francesca shuffled away with her tub of dishes and swimming eyes. Clicks began to follow her. But by the time Francesca finished struggling with the door to Orbel's Books, the sound of inappropriate shoes had faded.

28

SLOANE

She'd melded with a woman in a cloud of perfume and an obtrusive hat. The man sitting to her left had called her Gianna when he'd told her he thought they'd sung the last hymn. His dry, chapped fingers rubbed her palm–a familiar sensation, though false.

Gianna concentrated on the sermon; Sloane concentrated on not being expelled from Gianna.

Thirteen minutes and some odd seconds later to be almost exact, Gianna stood, but Sloane couldn't figure out how to follow.

Even after she'd been pushed out, Gianna's thoughts still lingered. She'd moved from the sermon to her husband and their marital bed. For a distinguished appearing woman, Gianna had dirty thoughts. Sloane had let those lead to one of her own sexual memories. A naked Francesca slid two fingers under Sloane's panties.

"Are you alright?" Molly asked.

Sloane calmed her heartbeat.

"Just trying to get to Francesca."

"Your face went slack and your eyes glassy like the children in my village did before they had fits. I was unaware that could happen in The Veil, though I will not pretend to know every-thing." Molly shrugged, and her ill-fitting dress slid off of her right shoulder.

"Hm," Sloane responded. Switching to a memory that wouldn't have her craving skin, Sloane honed in on the dimples that appeared when Francesca struggled not to laugh. She didn't think it would be strong enough, but it's what came up first.

A blink later, Sloane stood beside a sweating, swollen-eyed Francesca in her ugly pajamas with a knot of hair twisted up high on her head. With her knees curled under her, she sat with a box cutter in one hand. The other rested on an unopened box labeled, 'Shelf Four.'

Molly jumped onto the velvet three-person couch and made herself as solid as possible without being seen. If Francesca had been looking, she'd have screamed as the center cushion indented with Molly's force. Sloane's jealousy flared at her ability to do it without a thought.

"She has done an incredible job on this home."

Ignoring Molly, Sloane sidled up next to Francesca. Her hand shook as the knife slid through the tape like scissors through wrapping paper.

As Francesca popped open the box, she sighed. "Okay, Sloane, I hope I'm doing this right," she muttered.

"You are," Sloane whispered into Francesca's ear.

Her lips brushed pearl stud earrings that had been part of a scavenger hunt for their fifth year anniversary. Five clues, five presents, each better than the last, leading up to Sloane in a sweeping grey silk dress and the ballroom dance lessons she'd been mentioning since they'd been on their third date.

Francesca snapped her head and stared right at Sloane. Her breath caught. "Sloa–" Bursting into laughter, she grabbed a stack of books and stood. "A year later and you're still talking to her. Shouldn't you stop at some point?" she said aloud. "No, and you know, I don't want to. Hear that, love? I'm going to talk to you forever."

Francesca had always had a habit of talking to herself. The first time Sloane heard it, she had been coming home, and Francesca was in the shower. Heart sinking, she expected to find another woman in the bathroom with her. To her surprise, Francesca had her hands in her sudsy hair, chatting away in a normal tone of voice.

"Oh!" Her eyes were so wide, Sloane thought they'd fall out. "I... I'll be out in a few minutes."

They never did talk about it. It just became something Sloane expected. Talking to Sloane after she'd gone had been a logical step–almost a rational explanation for it.

Francesca mouthed each title as she placed them in order. "Damnit. Did you put *Greyson* by *The Cirque* because it's the same author, or were they organized by genre? Wait, it could have been alphabetized. How did you make our house so beautiful without any help? The bookshelves were so put together." Francesca's shoulders hunched and began to shake. "Maybe I should just make it look pretty. I don't read like you do." She sighed and corrected herself quietly, "Did." After a long pause, Francesca jumped up and ran to the bedroom. "Of course! I took pictures."

"This is a serious matter to her," Molly commented. "Who knew stacking books in a library could be so stressful."

"Me." Sloane sat in her reading chair out of normalcy, not out of need. "I spent days working on it–the one in San Francisco, that is. I put the books up to get them off the floor one day, then every day after that I tinkered. I'm glad she took pictures."

Francesca stomped back into the living room shaking her head. "I knew it seemed wrong! So much for putting things in the right boxes–thanks, guys. Okay." She rolled up the sleeves of

her wrinkled, stained button-up shirt. "One book at a time it
is then."

Molly reminded Sloane she was in fact just a child as she
whined, "We aren't going to sit here the entire time, are we?"

"You can do what you want," Sloane said. "I want to be here.
Besides, I have some thinking to do. I don't know why I couldn't
stand up with Gianna."

Molly said something, but Sloane's mind had already moved
on to the first time she'd seen Francesca dressed-down in the
ugly pajamas. They'd been together for a few months and had
decided to have a lazy Saturday where they were going to paint
each other's bodies, something Sloane had seen in The Pillow
Book. When she'd come over, Francesca had had messy hair,
worn the same makeup she'd worn from her girl's night out with
friends the night before, and the soon-to-be-infamous ugly pajamas. Sloane's dream of painting words on each other had flown
out the window. They'd painted little wooden trays which were
purely decorative, as they wouldn't hold but one small plate. She
wondered if her poorly designed beach scene had made it to
Montepulciano.

29

FRANCESCA

The first knock on Francesca's door involved a sweaty teenager with an odor she worried may linger on her doorstep holding apology daisies.

"I'm sorry I pushed,
  Cecelia"

The flowers brightened Francesca's mood a little. Maybe they could be friends. She'd spent the last two days putting books where they belong, sobbing, and ranting at Sloane; they'd helped her claw her way out of her darkness.

She went straight into the kitchen and looked for her vase covered in book pages to put them in. The rushing water from the sink refreshed her. It had been so long since anyone had given her flowers. They looked beautiful in the center of the living room with streams of colored light bouncing off the petals.

Francesca stared at the daisies as she called Cecelia. After four rings, it went to voicemail. "Hey! It's Cecelia Loreti, and I can't come to the phone right now. If you need me, leave me a message. If you want me, leave me a message. If you're bothering me, go away. Don't forget to leave your number, so I can call you back if I want to. Here comes the beep."

Smiling hard, Francesca didn't hang up in time, and the beep forced her to leave a message. "Hi, Cecelia, it's Francesca. I just called to say thank you so much for the daisies! It was so thoughtful of you. There was no need to apologize, but you are completely forgiven. How about we go for some dessert next week? Call me when you can, and we'll plan a day. Talk soon."

Her heart had been pounding so hard that after she hung up, she had to look down to make sure it wasn't visible. She'd just made a coffee date with Cecelia—no, not a date. A coffee... meeting?

MAMA ENJOYED DRESSING up a little for dinner, even mother-daughter dinners. For her mother, Francesca wore one of her striped maxi dresses. They'd become a favorite of hers as she didn't have to shave her legs, she looked taller, and she could dress them up or down.

They were the perfect dresses. Sloane would have mocked her mercilessly for how many colors she'd bought when Mama took her shopping. She wore no makeup and left her hair down. Mama should be pleased; Francesca looked semi-dressy.

The drive to her mother's place took about six minutes, which had Francesca arriving ten minutes early. She'd anticipated traffic, despite their homes being in view of each other.

"You came early! That's so sweet of you! Come on into the kitchen."

"Uh... So, how's my spaghetti coming along?"

When Mama had called the day before to invite her to dinner, she'd actually asked her what she wanted. Shocking—she had a say for once! Mama said she'd make other things too. "So that we have extras."

Francesca didn't know why they needed extras but assumed Mama didn't want spaghetti. She loved her mother.

Mama looked her up and down. "You look so beautiful and natural." Code: You aren't wearing makeup, and your clothes are plain.

"Thank you. My natural beauty comes from my mother." Francesca pretended not to notice the odd barb.

Eyebrows raised at her naked freckles, Mama asked, "Would you like some blush? Or lipstick perhaps?"

"Why would I need that, Mama? Am I hard to look at? We've have had many meals without me all painted." Trying to ignore the hurt, Francesca reminded herself that her mother often phrased things oddly, but meant them in entirely different–and benign–ways. She hoped that was one of them.

"Of course you aren't! I just thought when we turned the lights down you may pale a bit. I don't want anyone to think you're sick."

"Who's anyone?" A sinking feeling filled Francesca's stomach. Not at a mother-daughter dinner, it seemed.

"The Loreti's, Lia and Alonzo, Benito and Stefano Portera, and Benito's daughter, Gemma–you haven't met her yet. She lives just a few houses down. Maybe you two could be friends."

"What the hell are you talking about? I thought you and I were having dinner! Just you and me! You said, 'I haven't seen you in days.'"

"Well, I haven't. It just so happens I was having a dinner party tonight." Mama stirred the spaghetti sauce instead of looking at Francesca.

"Then why didn't you have me over yesterday, or I don't know, tell me about the people? You asked me what I wanted. Oh, Mama," Francesca said, as her smarts kicked in. "Cecelia is coming, isn't she?" Boiling water mirrored her bubbling irritation.

"Yes. But it's not a set-up; I have to invite her, and I worried you wouldn't come. I would have understood, of course. But..."

"I completely understand, I really do. You should have just told me." Francesca tore off a piece of un-toasted focaccia and stuffed it in her cheek. Through chewing, she told Mama, "She sent me flowers yesterday. They were to say sorry. I told her we'd see each other next week. But Mama, we are adults. I need you to talk to me as if you remember I'm an adult or this won't work."

"What won't work?" Her voice went high-pitched and panicky. "You living here? Oh, I'm so sorry, Essie! I should have. I was worried you wouldn't come. And I want you two to get used to being around each other. I shouldn't have done it this way. If you want to go, I understand. No one knows you're coming."

Francesca's legs twitched, but her head shook. Didn't she just say she was an adult? "No, I'm staying. What can I help with?"

Mama's eyes lit up. "Stir the fettuccine."

AFTER THE TABLE had downed ten bottles of wine, Mama turned on swing music. Benito asked Alma to dance. Her eyes twinkled as she agreed. Creases Francesca hadn't seen before appeared around her mouth.

Dancing on the lawn, they resembled the ever-rotating plastic couple in music boxes. Her ankle-length red and orange dress turned into a teacup of a circle, as they whirled in unison.

Tony announced, "They can't be the only ones, can they?" He stood and held his hand out to Gemma. "Would you care to dance?"

Stained purple lips slurred the words, "Of course."

Slightly younger than Tony, she probably shouldn't have matched him glass for glass.

Tony pulled her to a space a few steps away from his mother and Benito. Gemma's unbound long hair flew in her face with the first spin. She didn't bother pushing it back. Instead, she giggled and wiggled closer to Tony. He'd be tasting her shampoo in no time.

As if they were in a movie prom, Stefano set his wine glass down and stood quickly. He grinned at Mama and outstretched his hand. "Honor me?" he asked with a sultry voice.

Mama's face flushed. "That sounds nice, Stefano." She laced her fingers into his as he led her towards the other couples.

Alonzo followed by pulling his lovely Lia up and spinning her to the impromptu dance floor of Mama's yard. Lia laughed and threw her head onto his shoulder the moment they began dancing.

So familiar, they fell in step without a second of clumsiness.

The moon, the stars, and the glittering lights shifted the atmosphere to that of a wedding: jovial, loving, and filled with promise. Francesca knew she'd made the right choice when she moved to Montepulciano. Endless pasta and dinner parties—how had she'd lived without them? With a fleeting pang, she wished Sloane were there. Cecelia tore Francesca from her thoughts. "Don't worry."

"About what?" Swept up in the beauty of the laughter and dance in front of her, she had little worry.

"I wasn't going to ask you."

For some reason, that hurt Francesca, even though she probably would have panicked and said no. "Okay," she said.

"I didn't want to make you uncomfortable." She paused. "But in the spirit of the night, I changed my mind. Would you care to dance?"

A smile and blush had Francesca feeling heat where she

hadn't in a while. Her lips attempted to form the word no. Instead, she nodded. "Thank you for asking."

What?

Cecelia took the lead once they started dancing, and Francesca felt safe. Acutely aware of her hands, Francesca concentrated on a blurred light above the patio door flickering in and out of her sight as they twirled. The small of her back lit up, and they moved closer. Only for a moment, Francesca caught fire. It could have been the wine, the party, even the feel of Cecelia's warm body against hers, but she felt that one day she may be okay again.

Mama's face was a mask of questions as she met Francesca's eyes. Guilt exploded in her, but she didn't stop dancing. For once, Francesca wouldn't deny herself a small bit of temporary happiness. Instead, she leaned into it and tried to embrace the feeling of Cecelia's breath on her neck and how good it felt. Tears of disappointment in herself begged to fall but didn't.

She'd unpack the pain and self-loathing at home.

FRANCESCA HAD no idea what she wanted to do.

Starting over meant she could pick a new career. Or hell, she could work a mediocre job as if she were in high school again. A few of those had been fun. No matter how she sliced it, though, she had no clue where to start: help wanted signs, the internet, her mother?

She chose signs. Her list of to-dos including exploring the neighborhood anyway.

Hoping her Italian job search would be as easy as it was in the movies, Francesca wandered the streets looking for the sign that would lead her to the perfect job. The search had begun at 8 am and had gone on for two solid hours.

Seven blocks later, and she'd ended up with zero job prospects, three bags full of goodies, and a desperate need for a shower; hitting the pavement made her sweaty. Luckily, all of the busyness kept her from dwelling on the spot on her back that still tingled from Cecelia's hand.

With a lack of direction, Francesca did what any disheartened girl would do; she called her mother. "I need a job." Wait, wasn't she a woman? Too late to go back now.

"I know, Essie," Mama said. A clanging sound loudly covered the rest of her words.

"Everything okay over there?"

"Yes, just doing dishes. I didn't do them last night as I had intended."

Francesca said, "I understand. It was a great evening." Inside she gasped. Mama hadn't done the dishes; was she sick?

"It was. You and Cecelia looked like you were having fun," she said. "Go slow, Essie. Hearts are fickle." And here Francesca thought Mama might not bring that up.

"So, about the job..."

In the background, a man's voice called out. "My love, come back to bed. The dishes can wait."

What? One in the afternoon and a man—Francesca put the pieces together. Stefano Portera had stayed over. That explained the dishes; her mother rarely left dishes.

Francesca remembered an evening when extended family had kept them up until past midnight telling stories about when they were children. Though they were nothing-stories–the kind you share to pass the time in an airport if your layover is five hours–they told them as if they could end up at a storytelling festival. Francesca had only been fourteen, so Mama had been pissed. She was rarely allowed to stay up past eleven and only for special occasions.

Neither of them found that particularly special. After the

family had finally run out of even the most boring stories, despite the fact it had been one-thirty in the morning, Mama had cleaned.

"Oh, sorry, I didn't realize you were on the phone. I'll be waiting for you," he said.

Even if she couldn't have heard Mama's blush in her words–which she most certainly could–she'd have known it was there. "Uh, uh, I'm sorry, Essie. I've got to... I've, I'm so... Oh dear."

"Mama?" Francesca started. "Please take a breath. So Stefano stayed over? I'm happy for you. It sounds like maybe this isn't the first time, which is even better. Since he said he'll wait, though, let me ask you a quick question before you go back to your love bubble." Francesca wished she could've winked at her mother then.

She couldn't help but joke with Mama.

Mama's voice still shook. "Of course." Water cut off from the faucet followed by chair legs scraping.

Good, Francesca had her attention.

"I need a job, but my neighborhood doesn't have any signs that say they need help. Isn't that an anywhere-but-America thing? I saw it on TV." She was only half-joking.

"Oh, Essie," Mama laughed.

"I want something I'll enjoy. I don't mind if doesn't pay well, because two beautiful women bought me a house. I'm going to try and pay them back one day, though. But for now, I don't have rent. My car is paid off. I've got utilities, insurances, food, tv, my two credit cards, and fun. I'm sure I'm missing one or two things, but still. I don't need too much."

"You have credit card debt?" Mama asked in horror.

Francesca sighed. "Doesn't everyone?"

"No, I most certainly do not."

"I mean everyone who isn't rich, obviously."

"I'll pay it off; then you'll have one less thing. We'll talk about that tomorrow at dinner. How about you come over? We'll have a quiet evening, just you and me?"

"That's a hard no on you paying off my debt. I am an adult, you know. I can do *some* things for myself." Francesca sighed internally wondering if mentioning her credit cards had just earned her Emily Gilmore Sunday night dinners with wine and loud Italians. "But I'd love to come to dinner tomorrow night. Now, about that job?"

CECELIA CHEWED the last bite of her panini. Through a chipmunk cheek, she said, "I'm glad you called."

"I said I would."

"I didn't expect you to so soon. I was thinking a week or two, not a few days."

"So was I," Francesca admitted. Espresso steamed in front of her. "But after last night..."

She sipped her too-hot drink and let the words live between them.

In any other situation, they'd probably be on be their first date after the previous night's burgundy-mouthed spontaneity. Few moments held that kind of magic.

Francesca recalled a moment captured in a photograph stuffed in a drawer; with it out of constant view, she cried less. A few friends had come to help her and Sloane clean and re-stain the mini-deck behind their house slash bookstore. They'd made an adult play-date of it, complete with popsicles and a water hose. The popsicles had turned out great, all boozy and purple-flavored.

Harry, their long-time friend, had intended on soaking everyone with a high powered gush of warm water before they'd got down to work. When he'd faced the hose at them and twisted the knob, no rushing stream sprayed them; instead, a cascade of liquid sprinkles had misted over them.

Rachael had screamed at Harry to stand still as she'd run to grab the camera.

"Kiss her!" Rachael had shouted, pointing spastically at Sloane. Neither had known what was happening, but Sloane had laid one on Francesca.

At some point, the water had stopped raining on them, and Rachael had said, "I got it, guys." But they'd kissed on.

After Francesca had pulled away, she'd turned to Rachael. "What was that all about, anyhow?"

"You won't believe me until you see it! On a cloudy day, you two create a rainbow. Pure magic, I think. Only you guys could make that happen." She'd shaken her head and laughed; a hint of envy had lived behind it. Sloane and Francesca had often been the cause of that.

They'd run over to see the pictures and gasped. A rainbow, as if made only for them, hovered right above their heads. Sloane rarely framed photos, but she'd printed that one out the next day.

Francesca began thinking of more magical moments with Sloane: bright blue pool water and clumsy fingers, brick walls and bright lights, secret nibbles during phone calls, nights where she'd taught Sloane Italian.

Cecelia made a noise in agreement, and Francesca was in the present again. Cecelia held back a smile. Francesca wondered if she had any magic stories, but wouldn't ask. That may lead to a conversation Francesca wasn't ready to have. That may lead to leaning again. Francesca would love to get to know Cecelia, but not if they leaned.

"So, what did you want to do today?" Cecelia asked.

Francesca shrugged. Meeting her at lunch felt safe, but she hadn't thought there would be more than that.

Cecelia had an idea before Francesca's shoulders settled. "How about we head over to Lia's?"

"Mmm, sweets. I thought that was like an hour away?"

"Not even close—if you don't drive like our mothers. And besides, it *is* for sweets," Cecelia pointed out slyly.

Damn. She had a point.

Thirty minutes—not the fifty it took Mama—flew by with Cecelia. Listening to a story about the first time she'd picked grapes for the winery helped distract Francesca from the cold plastic-scented air blowing directly on her strappy lime sandals and Cecelia's lavender perfume.

"Sorry, that must have been boring. I just, I'm always trying to think of stories to tell you, but I always come up empty. You've lived this crazy life, and I've just been here."

Francesca nearly laughed. "In Italy."

"Yes, but not traveling much." Cecelia plugged in a little pine-scented air freshener. Could there be any more smells?

"Except for Europe."

"Yes, but not many other places."

"Cecelia, you underestimate your life, I think." Francesca felt dizzy.

"Maybe so." Cecelia went quiet. It seemed as though she was contemplating Francesca's off-handed comment on a deeper level than she'd meant it. Before she could shake herself out of her introspection, Lia's was in sight.

Cecelia had barely parked before Francesca escaped for a desperate attempt at relief.

"Francesca, look!" Cecelia shouted.

"What?"

"The sign in Lia's window—did you know she needed help?" She grabbed her hand and squeezed.

Francesca's heart soared.

"No, did you?"

Cecelia shook her head, still holding Francesca's hand. "Not at all! What a happy accident!"

Taking a small step towards the building, Francesca broke Cecelia's grip. She didn't seem to notice in her excitement.

"Do you think you'd work here?"

"For free sweets, of course. But it's a bit of a drive, and what does Lia even need? It's not as if I know how to make bread. If I did, I'd be 300 pounds, at least. No joke."

Francesca pictured a life where she kneaded dough, wore a linen apron and a tea towel over her shoulder, had flour on her nose, the whole deal. Sloane slid her arms around her from behind and tried to knead with her. She nearly sighed at how easily the image came.

With Sloane alive, anything seemed possible.

Without, Francesca saw herself alone with wet dough, wearing her ugly pajamas in a disaster of a kitchen.

Cecelia chuckled. "I'll ask!"

"I think I can do that."

"I really don't mind," Cecelia said.

She had fallen into girlfriend mode too quickly, despite her lack of being appointed the role. Cecelia needed to slow to new-friend mode.

Lia peeked through the large picture window filled with loaves of bread, flanked by picture boxes overflowing with colorful flowers.

Stepping out, she motioned for them to come in. "Ladies! It's so good to see you both again. Come in out of the heat. How are you doing? Can I get you anything?"

"A job?" Francesca half-joked.

"You're looking?" Lia's perfectly sculpted eyebrows shot up. "I had no idea! I'd love some help. I can't pay much, but you can have all the free desserts you want."

What had she just said? "So far so good."

"Let's talk business then. Have a seat." Pouty lips pursed as Lia pointed at a small bistro table set in the corner. "I'll go get the paperwork, and we can hash the details out."

"Seriously? That easy?"

Lia took a sign Francesca hadn't noticed down from the window. "Seriously." Smiling, she sauntered into the back room before coming out with a pen and a stapled packet of paper.

"I told you," Cecelia said, nudging Francesca. "I'm so proud of you."

Hearing that had Francesca's chest pounding with a nameless emotion. Sloane used to say that about small things too. No one else cared that much, probably not even Mama.

Shit.

Two days before her first shift at the bakery Francesca had a few hours of unpacking left. The still-taped boxes dared her to ignore them again. Resisting the urge to yell at the helpless cardboard, she grabbed a bottle of wine and steeled herself.

Within hours, purposefully ignored captured moments had been spread across the living room floor. Sloane's records filled the space. Only novelty lights illuminated the house: three sets of white Christmas tree lights, a restored stolen exit sign, a naked Edison bulb with twisted filament, and a set of plastic flamingos. Francesca held onto a book like a lifeline. She was too drunk to read its title, but it was Sloane's; that mattered more than the words on the pages.

Thoughts of Sloane were scabs itching to be ripped open. Francesca herself short of delving into any one memory.

A KNOCK WOKE A HUNGOVER FRANCESCA. Sitting up proved to be painful and sad; a photograph of Sloane kissing her left laughing cheek stuck to her swollen, drool-covered right one. The knock sounded again, more insistent. Mama better have a good reason for waking her up. She had another day before adult life kicked in.

Cecelia stood in her doorway with wet hair in a put together outfit. Wasn't it too early to be out of bed? Francesca blinked away the film still covering her eyes, casually rubbing the gunk away.

"Rough night?" Cecelia smirked.

Francesca coughed. "Something like that. What's up?"

"Can I come in?"

Francesca stuttered in answer.

Cecelia blushed. "Unless someone is—"

"No! It's just I went through some stuff last night. Come on in." Francesca rushed to the floor and scrambled to stack the photographs and love notes. "Sorry."

"Why? I think it's wonderful you have these. Do you want to show me some?" Long legs kneeled to glance at the collection.

Flabbergasted, Francesca stared at the love in her hand. Could she share these with anyone? Could she share them with Cecelia? Before she could even make a decision, Cecelia held a photograph, her jaw tight.

Cecelia sat on the peach velvet couch Francesca had just found at an antique store. "Is this her?"

Their second Halloween flashed back in snapshots like the ones scattered on the carpet. Sloane wouldn't dress up, so Francesca had been a lonely Scarecrow who'd found her Lion and Tin Man at a bar with a drunken Dorothy; their Scarecrow had had to bail for some reason or another. Sloane might as well have been the Wicked Witch she'd been green. Jealousy had never suited them. They'd left early to go home and watch horror movies. Every year after, Sloane dressed up to the nines– couples costumes only.

"Yes, that was Halloween. She wasn't one for costumes in the beginning."

Emotions splattered Cecelia's face like a Pollock. "She was beautiful."

Francesca nearly corrected her with, 'She is beautiful.' "I am a lucky woman," she said instead. It just slipped out, and Cecelia looked crestfallen.

"What about this one?" She reached over a stack to point at a Polaroid.

Sloane and Francesca stood in short 80s-styled dresses. Teased hair and over-done makeup made them look like entirely different people. If it weren't for Sloane's hair and eyebrows, she could have been any 80s pop star.

"Adult Prom. We went every year. I used to love any excuse to dress up, and this one was great. This was from the first year. She knew the guitarist from the cover band. I can't remember who they covered usually, but they sang Cindi Lauper all that night." Francesca remembered how Sloane had danced to "Girls Just Want To Have Fun". "My feet were covered in blisters from wearing those ridiculous shoes. I swore I'd never wear heels to any event again." She scrunched her face holding back laughter.

Cecelia tossed wet hair into a quick bun. "I take it you broke your promise?"

"Of course! Costumes dictate my footwear, don't they?"

"You're adorable," Cecelia said, her eyes glittering. Quickly, she turned her attention back to the scattered photographs. Stacking them, she stopped on another. "Whoa! What's this?"

Sloane was on one knee, and Francesca's hand was over her mouth.

"That's a photo we took for my friend's portfolio. She'd wanted to pretend she caught the 'Will you?' moment. It had been hard for Sloane because I'd already told her we didn't need to get married. We never had a wedding, which I know she wanted; I robbed her of that."

Reaching out, Cecelia took Francesca's hand. "Looking at these pictures, I can tell you had a beautiful life. A wedding would have been great, but she had you, and I know that was enough. How could it not be?"

Francesca couldn't tilt her head up; it felt dangerous–she was too vulnerable.

"So, uh–I just came by to ask if you needed a ride to work for your first week at Lia's? I don't mind. Admittedly, it's not on the way to my job, but I've already talked to them about it. I said 'family,' so they'd be okay with it. I know you don't have a car yet. You don't have to, of course. I just thought I'd offer. So–" Cecelia floundered.

Francesca put her out of her misery. "Thank you. I'd really appreciate that."

"Alright. What time should I pick you up?"

"My shift starts at 9, so how's 8:15?"

Cecelia stood and headed out. "How's 7:45? We can grab breakfast."

"Sure."

"Great. It's a date." She slammed the door on her words, leaving Francesca with the word 'date'.

30

FRANCESCA

Three Weeks Later

When the last customer left Lia's, Francesca melted into the counter. The sharp metal edges cut into her ribs, a painful reminder that she couldn't rest yet. The bakery had to be cleaned from top to bottom and prepped for Lia's morning bake.

Francesca boxed up the few remaining baked treats.

As Lia put it, "The leftover goodies have to be well taken care of: no cleaners near them, tightly wrapped, etc." Her stern voice was adorable. "I always sell out of my 'day-olds'. People feel like they're getting a discount, and the food still tastes delicious. Win-win."

Francesca placed each into the beautiful basket with a calligraphy label, then got to work.

The smell of blue cleaner replaced the swirling fresh bread and cinnamon raisin scent Lia's usually held. As if she were cleaning a crime scene, Francesca wiped away fingerprints and crumbs left on the counter by eager customers.

She pulled out display trays covered in broken pieces of

chocolate and dustings of powdered sugar and took them to the large sink in the back. The size of the stainless steel tub reminded her of the only time she'd been to a stable. Sloane had taken her to ride a horse–a bucket list item. The owner of the horse had walked them through a day in the life of owning a horse. Educational, exhausting, a little gross, yet somewhat fun.

Water from the large power-hose bounced off of a pan and spritzed her in the face. Her favorite sweet topping had become a gummy substance as she'd wandered into la-la-land. Francesca wanted to lick it, but a pattern had developed.

She had gained a pound every week she'd been at Lia's–three and counting. Unless she wanted to buy yet another new wardrobe, she needed to learn a little restraint. Besides, licking the tray would be a low point in her sweet-eating career.

Before she'd finished drying off the trays, before she'd gotten to sweeping or mopping, before she'd prepped for Lia's morning, the store bell chimed.

"Just me." Cecelia's voice echoed through the empty store. "Am I early?"

"By forty-five minutes. But you knew that," Francesca replied.

There was no need to hurry, or even go in the front to say hello. The scraping sound told Francesca Cecelia had already made herself comfortable in one of the trios of chairs by the shelves that held various bread loaves each morning.

Cecelia said the words Francesca heard nearly every day since her first day of work, "I'll just read a few chapters then. Take your time."

Francesca continued her cleaning, while Cecelia read her 'smut'.

Cecelia recounted the highlights to Francesca in fifteen-minute catch-up sessions. Lacey may finally make a choice this coming chapter; Francesca was hoping for Ashley, but Cecelia shipped Rachael.

Cleaning took thirty minutes, down from forty-five as Francesca had streamlined her routine.

Her heart did a small pitter-patter–as it always did–when she walked out to see Cecelia. Most days Cecelia carried her long hours with her: mussed hair and stained overalls.

But when Francesca made her way to the front of the store, Cecelia's hair was silky and straightened. Apparently, she'd gotten off of work early. She wore tight jeans, ballerina flats, and a low-cut shirt.

Francesca's stomach tightened, and Cecelia's blue bra flashed in her mind. A gust of imaginings filled her head. Forcing her eyes towards the setting sun, she breathed deeply.

She owed Sloane an apology. Again.

"HOW ARE YOU DOING?" Mama asked before she closed the door behind her.

"Come on in, Mama. Take your shoes off, and stay a while." Francesca hid her smile by walking towards the kitchen. Surprise visits had become less of a surprise.

"So, how are you doing?"

"Water, Mama?"

"Yes. Tap is fine. You look nice." Mama plopped on the couch temporarily abandoning the question.

Francesca wandered back in with two tall clear glasses filled to the brim with cold water. "Okay, hello. I'm fine, Mama, thanks. Dinner out tonight. No, we aren't dating." Suddenly self-conscious, Francesca wished she had a mirror to check her pulled back twist for flyaways. Her lipgloss felt intact.

Mama stared at the grey and white flowered tea-length dress Francesca wore. "So you say." Narrowed eyes and a pursed mouth didn't believe a word.

"We aren't. She and I are spending a lot of time together, true. But I still love Sloane. I miss her every day." Would it help or hurt her cause if she stomped her foot?

"Essie, my darling, I never thought that changed. You will always love and miss Susan. If you find comfort in someone, though, it's okay to enjoy it. As long as you don't jump in; you still have to protect your heart."

"It's only been a year."

Mama's face was unreadable. She tucked a loose strand behind her ear and took a swig of water before she grabbed Francesca's hand.

"One week, one month, one year, one decade, never, that isn't what matters. Your heart has been broken in a way most people can't even fathom. If Cecelia can help heal it, even if it's only a little or temporary, then let her. Like I said, I'm not saying jump in. I'm not saying get married. I'm just telling you to stop judging yourself for the way you grieve and heal."

"I will never get married," Francesca replied as if that was the only bit she retained from her mother's lovely sentiment. How could she not hate herself?

"Okay, Essie. But think about what I said."

A loud horn sounded through one of the six open windows.

Squeezing her mother's hand, she asked a burning question. "You didn't love bio-dad, even though you were with him. It was always George, wasn't it?"

Mama shook her head quickly, untucking her strategically placed curls. "I did love him, just never like I did George. I've known people to feel the same way about multiple people, though. Head-over-heels-love happens without asking our permission. Why? Are you falling for Cecelia?"

"No, I'm not. But I am falling in 'like.' I'm feeling things I didn't think I could–ever wanted to–again, and that scares the hell out of me." The waterfall of truth tumbled out with no warning.

Mama pulled Francesca onto her shoulders and patted her head. "Shh, my Essie. It's going to be okay. Whatever happens is supposed to, you know that. It will turn out as it should. And no matter what, Susan would want you to be happy."

"Would she?" Francesca would want Sloane to be happy too, but in the arms of another woman?

"Ye–" A loud knock at the door interrupted Mama's reassurances.

"That's her. We are having dinner tonight." Hot shame filled Francesca.

Mama looked pleased, though. "Well, I'll just head out then."

"You don't have to go! She's early, so she can–"

"Essie, it's fine. You have some figuring out to do." Mama went up on tiptoes, kissed Francesca on the cheek, and scurried to the door. "Hi, Cecelia. I was on my way out. Nice to see you."

Cecelia sputtered, "You don't have to leave! I'm early."

"So Essie told me. Have a good night. I'll see you both next week."

"Ready to go, doll?" Cecelia asked, eyes drinking Francesca in. "You look amazing!"

Gulp.

SIPPING lukewarm water did nothing for her nerves. A ring Sloane had bought from a bubblegum machine with a quarter she found on the sidewalk clinked against the glass. Francesca chastised herself for wearing it. Cecelia didn't know the story behind it; she could only see the scratched up turquoise plastic bobble. She probably naively thought it was a childhood memory. Francesca was always hiding.

"Have you two decided?" Their usual waitress was absent and replaced by a young man with speckles of stubble above his top lip. He fussed with his dark bed-head styled hair as if to say, 'Well?' when it took them more than a second to respond.

Cecelia nodded. "I have. Francesca, do you want your usual?"

They'd had dinner at the low-key restaurant a few times in the past month. It had always had a girls-dinner vibe until an hour ago. Cecelia showed up in a slinky black dress and red lipstick instead of her usual skirt and nice top combo.

"Without a doubt," Francesca replied. The words came out easily, felt so familiar. It wasn't until the waiter had walked away that she realized what she'd just said.

Silver ballet flats were the worst shoes she could have picked. Tennis shoes would have made her dash to the bathroom much quicker and smoother. Maybe she wouldn't have knocked into the hostess on her break or pushed open the door to the kitchen. The rug might not have tripped her either. Alas.

As Francesca sat on the floor outside of the restroom, her ankle blossoming in pain, panic gave way to tears. Patrons of the tiny, dim restaurant watched her as if she were a car accident. The thought stole her breath.

She didn't notice Cecelia sitting beside her until she rubbed warm circles on her back. "What happened?"

Francesca felt nauseous.

"Don't."

Cecelia's hand melted away with the sting of rejection.

"I'll call Mama Nuccio," she muttered and left Francesca in the half-hallway; her absence was a cold spot.

What seemed like years later, Mama appeared like an angel. Her small body wrapped around Francesca in a hug before she stood her up. "Let's get you home for some hot cocoa, wine, and a good cry."

"Mama, I said, 'Without a doubt.'"

She almost gave into another looming sob but wanted to hear Mama's thoughts too much.

"In the car. It sounds like we have a lot to talk about, you and me."

As they wandered out of the restaurant, Mama nodded at numerous tables–fantastic, she knows these people. None of it seemed to bother her, even in her silk PJs and socked feet.

"You could have changed, put on shoes." Francesca heard her pathetic voice and nearly laughed. She sounded so convincing.

Mama clucked. "No, Essie. If you'd have heard Cecelia... I had a split second of deciding whether I had time to put on PJs at all." Francesca attempted to keep her eyebrows neutral "It was clear you needed Mama. So I came, in all my glory. So." She paused as they settled into the car. "You said, 'Without a doubt,' to Cecelia. What brought that on?"

"Food. Goddamned food. She asked me if I wanted my usual. It felt so normal, so easy. There was some so comfortable about it that the phrase seemed okay to say. I'm wearing this ring and was thinking about Sloane two-seconds before she asked. Everything was so jumbled. It's not like I thought she was Sloane, but... I don't know. I never thought I'd be able to say that phrase again. Then, I did. This is what happened. I shouldn't be going out with Cecelia. I know where we could be heading–our mutual like. But she's no Sloane."

Francesca twisted her fingers together. Mama squished hers between and held Francesca's hand tightly. A few tears trickled down her face, but she stayed quiet for the remainder of the ten-minute drive home.

As they pulled into the parking lot Francesca used as her carport, she asked, "How about an ice cream slumber party... unless you have a guest at home?" Francesca wondered if she ruined her mother's night.

"I sent him home with a bottle of red and a container of

pasta. He'll be fine. He just wants you to be okay. I do have to call him and let him know how you're doing. Is that alright?"

"Of course. You two are serious huh? I'm going to have a new daddy?" Francesca smiled, and it felt good.

No answer followed. Instead, Mama started talking on the phone at rapid speed. Good, he could keep up with her; maybe he was a keeper after all. Francesca decided not to mention it again. She'd let Mama tell her when she was ready.

With that one moment of clarity, Francesca composed a text to Cecelia. "I'm sorry. I need a few days. I'm going to try and take a few days off work too. Maybe next week we could talk?"

Was that good enough? No. Was that too much to ask? Yes.

She sent it anyway.

"You ready for ice cream?" Mama popped in to see Francesca holding her phone. "What did you do, Essie?"

"What I thought I had to."

"Okay." Mama couldn't hide the worry lines that aged her forehead. "What flavor ice creams do you have?" Leave it to Mama to try and avoid with food.

IGNORING the call she received from Cecelia left a sour taste in her mouth. Words stuck in her throat begging to be spoken. Still, she listened as Cecelia left an awkward message–never more glad she had a home phone. Hadn't they done this already? Francesca wondered if the familiarity of dodging her was a sign.

"Hey. No need to answer or anything, I just called to say take your time. I think I'm accidentally pushing–again. So I'm going to take a step back. I'm sorry. You call me when you're ready. I– I'll m–Hopefully, I'll hear from you."

Francesca replayed the short voicemail three times.

Cecelia had wanted to say she'd missed her. The feeling would be mutual–the crux of the problem.

Sloane lived with Francesca; she wasn't sure there was any room left for Cecelia.

Her few days off flew by, and the monotony of a busy work week had the following days fly by without extra dwelling on Cecelia. Francesca began to see what living by herself felt like again, now that some of the clouds had parted. She avoided dinners and calls from everyone, including Mama.

As an adult, she'd always had someone. Before Sloane, there had been Theresa. Resa had consumed Francesca from the start, which felt a lot like love. Before Resa, she'd loved and lived with Polly–a secret polygamist. Before Polly, she had a slew of one night stands with women and men she'd met bar hopping.

Francesca hadn't been alone much before. Francesca felt alive and miserable.

On her first day off, without a second thought, she called Cecelia.

Cecelia's sultry voice came over the line. "Francesca?"

"Hi."

"How are you? We've been worried." Francesca knew Cecelia had curled her knees into her chest. In some ways, Cecelia and Sloane were so alike.

Trying not to sigh, Francesca said, "I've been working and trying to learn how to be an adult without another human around me all the time. I haven't lived alone, except for after Sloane, since I moved out of Mama's house. From girlfriend to girlfriend and friends in between, it just never really happened. After Sloane, I hardly felt alone. She was there. I felt her there always. Here, I feel her, but not in the same way. She never took a breath here, never laughed or cried here; it just has her things and my memories. So here I am fully alone."

A knickknack fell off the shelf again.

At first, Francesca had believed it to be Sloane communicating with her. But after many conversations with the air around her, she knew Sloane had truly gone away. Her bookshelf, though, seemed to be haunted. Mama had leered at it, the first time it happened. Still, they'd rationalized it away, like she did as it interrupted her pouring her heart out.

"What was that?" Cecelia sounded far away, and a slam in the background punctuated her question.

"Am I on speaker phone?"

"Yes. I'm grabbing some cereal. It's the real dinner of champions, you know." She chuckled at herself. A distinct suction noise followed. "The box says so, or it used to. Or was that the American commercial?" Cecelia put on an announcer's voice when she said, "This cereal is made of cardboard and sugar, but you should feed it to your growing children! Thank us later!"

Francesca laughed. "I think it was the commercial with the little boy. Isn't he the one who ended up in rehab?" The moment for sharing had passed. Hopefully, Cecelia understood enough to see why Francesca hadn't called her back. "So, I was calling because–"

"Crap. I don't have but one and a half bowls of milk left." A cabinet slammed. "Sorry, you were telling me about how you haven't been alone before." Cecelia sounded slightly out of breath and distracted.

"Oh, I told you everything." Francesca shut down. "Anyhow, I was calling because I wanted to see if you could pick me up from work again? Getting a taxi has been very expensive lately."

"Of course." Her disappointment almost melted the phone.

"And have dinner after?"

Cecelia perked right up. "Absolutely."

No.

Francesca's lips still tingled from the kiss Cecelia had brushed against the crook of her mouth. She'd just left, barely driven away. Why were Francesca's hands shaking from anything but excitement?

The words that Tony spewed through the phone had left her head spinning.

They'd finally had a successful date that didn't end in Francesca crying or running away.

It had been the second-best first date Francesca had ever been on. Their conversation had bounced from topic to topic, but with every one, Cecelia had sparkled like the chandelier above them.

She'd enthusiastically recounted the last few chapters of an erotica novel she'd bought two days ago. Francesca had loved every bit of it, despite that fact it sounded terrible; reading it wouldn't have had the same entertainment value Cecelia's retelling did, though.

"So, Lori throws Kelly against the wall. You think this is it; finally, they are going to have sex. But no, Thomas charges in and kills the mood. What kind of male walks in on lesbians and doesn't encourage sex? The least he could have done was turn around and leave, but no. No, he doesn't do that; he decides to start talking to Lori about some dumb paperwork. Nothing sexy about paperwork," Cecelia had lamented.

"I suppose there isn't. Does that mean you want Kelly and Lori to be together?"

Cecelia had shaken her head. "Absolutely not. Lori should be with Ashley from the book before this one. I know you wanted her to be with Theresa, but they aren't right for each other."

"I didn't even know this was a series."

"Oh yes! There are fourteen books and counting. The last

four books—before the last one—were duds. Thomas tried to date..."

Tony's voice broke through. "She's at St. Marco's Medical Center."

Since he'd said the word "accident," an image of a broken Sloane hovered at the edge of Francesca's thoughts.

When he added the hospital's name, she stuttered. "I– I–"

"Do you need a ride? I can have someone pick you up?" Francesca imagined the shaken Tony pacing in the waiting room as he called person after person. His hair was probably in knots from tugging. "I know she was just there."

'We only had one glass of wine!' Francesca nearly screamed.

She tried to move, but it was as if Medusa had stared her straight in the eyes. One foot hovered slightly above the floor as she stood in the bathroom focusing unblinkingly at the ruffled shower curtain. Partially cracked, she saw the flipped open shampoo bottle cap. It explained the overwhelming salon smell. Francesca wished she could look anywhere but the curtain.

The mirror would only hold the horror of her face. The floor was unswept; long black hair would have turned her stomach. A bouquet of flowers hung from her deep purple walls.

"–swerved. It was a freak accident. The other driver died before the ambulance showed up. Cecelia's still out, so they only have witnesses to tell them what happened. One woman on the street thinks the other driver saw a squirrel or something. A fucking squirrel. Can you believe it?" His attempt to laugh turned into heavy, uneven breaths. "I've got to go. Are you sure you can make it here on your own?"

"Me?" Finally, Francesca blinked. "Yes, I can. I can get there." No longer connected to her body, her head bobbed and weaved.

"If you need us, call," Tony said before the line went quiet.

Francesca had to focus all of her energy on putting on

sandals. When Mama's number showed up on the phone, she didn't bother answering.

Francesca drove like an old woman, ten kilometers under the speed limit–despite her desire to speed–out of fear. Slowly bruising hands clutched the wheel.

"Dear God, don't let Cecelia die," Francesca prayed aloud. "I know I only talk to you when I want or need something, but isn't that how it works? Fuck. You took Sloane; don't take Cecelia." She thought to curse him, but her silent curses were heard plenty loud enough.

As she neared the glowing red and white emergency sign, flashbacks of screams covered in blood rushed back.

She had little memory of driving, parking, or walking to the front desk, but she managed. The fog began to lift as she asked for Cecelia. The second elevator on the left dropped her off at the end of a stark hallway.

She followed it as though it were a white rabbit.

Words on signs had become symbols; Francesca may have forgotten Italian, she couldn't be sure.

A third hallway led her to a waiting room filled with more people than the average house party. Mounted high in the corner, an old TV quietly played a soap opera with a witch and triplets. Francesca thought her mother watched that one. One of the triplets was in a coma, but stable–how utterly predictable, and too close.

Alma and Tony saw her and rushed forward. Finally, the tears hovering behind her eyes spilled out.

"The family." Alma motioned to the room. Though her voice barely raised when she introduced Francesca, Alma commanded the room's attention.

For the next few moments, her lack of breath had nothing to do with worry or pain. Tight squeezes from strangers came from all angles. As if she were family, they all gave her condolences before going back to their prayers and tears.

It struck her that Sloane didn't have that kind of emotion at her funeral. A few friends had come in cheap, worn dresses used for all occasions and rolled-out-of-bed hair. Harry had worn an ill-fitted suit and eaten a lot of cheese at the modest wake that was all Francesca could afford. He hadn't seemed broken up about it. Rachael hadn't shown up. An only vaguely recognizable woman at the funeral had told her Rachael was at a pool party. Francesca had promptly excused herself to throw up.

Shakily, vomit still on her breath, Francesca had given the eulogy. If anyone had understood her through the hiccups and gagging, they must have been able to read lips. No one else said anything, which had Francesca wanting to spit on each one of the *mourners*. To hell with them.

She hoped Sloane had been spared from seeing the reality of their supposed friends. Cecelia wouldn't need to be spared. No matter the outcome, she had love. When the doctor came out, a hush covered them like a blanket.

He said what any good television doctor would. "She's lost a lot of blood, but we've done what we can for now. She's stable but in a coma. Now we just have to wait."

Wailing surrounded Francesca, cries of gratitude and pleas to God. The rest of the doctor's information seemed unimportant to the family.

Alma spoke above the familial chaos. "We'll be here until that happens. We'll take shifts, but we'll be here."

"I understand. But as I said, it could be–"

Her eyes narrowed as she cut him off with a spitting poison. "We'll be here."

~

THE BAKERY RAN at a steady pace, which kept Francesca's mind from staying in the hospital room. She slid into a rhythm revolving around nightly visits to see Cecelia. A new kind of grief flooded her.

Every memory, every thought, lead Francesca to pain.

On the fifth night of sameness: stories Cecelia couldn't hear, forehead kisses she couldn't feel, and hand squeezes she couldn't return, the doctor had news.

Francesca had arrived at the hospital at 6:40 pm. At 6:45 pm, Alma stood in the hallway and called for Tony. He tugged a piece of his hair out of the ponytail it'd been in for days. His nerves were fried.

Out of the corner of her eye, Francesca saw the doctor gently touch Alma's shoulder; with a blink and a nod, she crumpled soundlessly.

After a moment between Tony and Alma—one so touching Francesca had to turn away—they walked into the sterile, beeping room tall and strong.

Francesca met Alma's eyes and knew but had to hear the words to be sure.

"Essie," Alma said, her voice quivering. No one but Mama was allowed to call her that—usually. Perhaps her childhood nickname was meant to calm her, but there wouldn't have been a way to soften the blow. "I thought I should be the one to tell you. Cecelia's brain has stopped working—sorry, 'functioning'. They said there was nothing they could do. She was doing fine, then she—"

Her knees gave way away. Tony barely caught her before they cracked onto the hard hospital floor. She still grazed it, though didn't seem to notice. Francesca had a phantom pain from her still-green knee.

Francesca swallowed and blinked away the oncoming darkness; it wasn't her time to cry. Kneeling down, she clutched

Alma's hand. "Alma, you don't need to say that ever again if you don't want to." Francesca remembered what a gut punch it had been for her. Every time she'd told another person about Sloane, a little part of her soul had fallen away. "I can do it for you."

A different kind of crying overwhelmed Alma–a grateful kind. "I'm so glad Cecelia got to have you for as long as she did; you are remarkable. I couldn't appreciate the offer more. But this isn't yours to handle. I have a great deal of family to contact, and we have plenty to discuss before tomorrow."

"Tomorrow?" Francesca gulped. Too soon.

No one could replace Sloane, but Cecelia had helped fill the void in a way she'd never imagined anyone ever could again. Now she'd have a second void.

"Her soul is gone." Alma had such surprising composure it felt practiced. "We cannot leave her body like this. I'll give the family one day to say their goodbyes to her body if they so wish, then we will allow ourselves to grieve."

An attempt at her usual pragmatic self, Alma had it all planned as if it were an appointment. Monday we visit the shell of our family member, Tuesday we let it die, Wednesday we feel, Thursday, what? Do they plan the funeral for the shell?

Francesca tried not to–she begged her insides–but she fell apart. In no way should she be the one being comforted, but Alma's arms surrounded her. Tony leaned over and kissed the top of her head. The love they shared with her helped about as much as hearing her nickname.

A shout broke the silence. "I'm so sorry I wasn't here!" Mama had a near-collision with a nurse as she bounded down the hall.

Alma just opened an arm for Mama.

Tony broke the silence as he said, "I love you" to Cecelia.

31

SLOANE

With a freedom Sloane was finally beginning to harness, she traveled through the hospital and observed moments where time would be moving as slowly as it had the day she'd died. A man slumped in the corner of the room yanked at his hair.

He stared intently at the two small children who sat on the edge of a brunette woman's bed. She had bright blue smeared eyeshadow up to her eyebrows and hot pink blush in a circular pattern on her cheekbones.

The smallest child, a blonde girl no older than five, held a makeup palette and wore a smile. Nurses rotated in as if they were doing a revolving door bit; only no one laughed. Sloane tried not to listen, but the nurse in bunny and carrot scrubs whispered "three days, at best" to a nurse wearing only plain blue on their way out of the room.

On a different floor, a woman held an unconscious man's limp hand. Alone, they were a faded photograph.

A female doctor with a purple stethoscope came in and asked if she wanted to call anyone–he'd be out for a while. But neither had any family; she was all he had. A pile-up on the highway, it seemed.

"Just keep him comfortable," the doctor told a nearby nurse. "When he wakes up from surgery, he'll have nothing to look forward to but pain and a worried wife. Both are very stressful."

After several more rooms and hallways and floors of family pain, Sloane found Francesca in a restroom near Cecelia's room.

Splashing her face with water, Francesca whispered to her mirror self. "Hold it together. You only have to make it home before you fall apart. You don't have a choice. You need to get some sleep. There's nothing you can do for her." She dried her hands on her jeans and tied her hair up. "Sloane, I wish you were here."

Francesca seemed confused by her own words, but she opened the bathroom door and stepped out without looking back into the mirror.

Francesca would be okay soon.

Soon, they'd be together. Sloane kept reminding herself of that.

MOURNERS FILLED CECELIA'S ROOM. Sloane hovered in the corner by Molly. Minutes until Sloane would have a window, she asked Molly what happened, even though she wasn't sure she wanted to know.

"An opportunity presented itself." Molly giggled.

Sloane's entire body temperature flashed, despite The Gray having no breeze and her having no internal fluids. Feeling like a wrung out shirt, Sloane tried to focus on the amazing future she and Francesca were about to have and not the spots of blood on her hands that would never wash.

The doctor began his speech.

"You may hear some sounds after I unplug the machines; they may even resemble breathing. Those are nor–"

Sloane checked out of the doctor's rehearsed speech to focus on her own, the one she'd planned to give the day she died. "Are you sure you can get it?" she asked Molly.

"Of course. You focus on melding, and I will see you soon."

"Will you? I mean, will we see each other?" The thought of never seeing Molly again brought mixed emotions.

Sloane could hear her stopped heart beat. The machine had been turned off, and silence had taken hold. Cecelia's mother and brother held each hand of her shell. The Gray's blurred filter became weighted, heavy as if anticipating a soul's attempt to shatter through.

"Never mind all of that now; it is time!" Molly urged. "Go!"

Francesca's lips came into focus, as Sloane sat on Cecelia's bed. She thought she had a strong enough memory, but she faltered; fragments of their life together, their love, struggled to become whole.

A small but beautiful moment popped into her head. Sloane hoped it would be enough.

December 22nd, two years ago, Francesca had squeezed Sloane's hand as they stood in line for the mall Santa. Sloane had always wanted to go and take a photo on Santa's lap, but her childhood had been a waste. As she'd grown older, she had become a Scrooge.

Francesca and Sloane had been binging the entire series of both Buffy the Vampire Slayer and Angel when Francesca paused abruptly and said, "Go get dressed! We're going to see Santa."

Groaning, Sloane had known whatever she'd say next would be useless. It wasn't as if Francesca hadn't had random moods or desires that led to adventures before. They'd almost always come at the worst time–such as in the middle of a TV marathon at 6 pm. "It's late and cold. Not to mention my hair is a mess, and I'm comfy. Besides, are you sure you want to brave the mall a few days before Christmas?"

"It's not late, you old woman, you. It's not that cold, either. I'll fix your hair in ten minutes or less, and you can be comfy again when we come home. We'll have cocoa." Francesca had grabbed a hairband from the side table, a twinkle in her eye. Of course one had been handy when Sloane was resistant to doing something.

"And braving the mall?"

"Will suck. But it's part of the experience. You know, getting irritated at shitty parents, wanting to punt a small child across the room to shut it up, hating the smell of play-dough, but also wanting to buy some because it's fun and making things you can smush is satisfying."

Sloane had felt old as she stood up from the couch. "Wow, you make it sound like so much fun."

Francesca had given her a perfect toothy smile and kissed Sloane's cheek. They were going. Despite her resistance, Sloane had known before they left that she'd have fun. Didn't she always?

Standing in line had been exactly what Francesca had said it would be: a child-filled hell that ended in her wanting to shop at Toys-R-Us. They'd both agreed they'd do that next, though they were both pre-grumpy about the whole–

Sloane felt a push she hadn't experienced when melding with someone. With no soul there to share the body with, she'd expected sliding in would be easy. Then she felt it: Cecelia had come back to fight. She must have been in The Gray–not gone–the entire time.

Panicked, disjointed thoughts bounced around Sloane. Cecelia wished she could move on but wanted to come back too. Sloane decided to push once more. If there was any resistance, then Cecelia was meant to stay. With a relieved sigh, Sloane felt Cecelia's hold melt and slip away. Sloane imagined dancing with Francesca again, feeling her skin. Lyrics from The Monologue Bombs echoed in her head like a soundtrack to the moment. "The memory of your skin, I block it out. It comes back in. Laughter sang. Luna shone. We were home."

A scream rippled inside as Sloane claimed Cecelia's body. The pain became vocal, and for the first time in over a year, someone besides Molly could hear Sloane.

32

FRANCESCA

Francesca's low back throbbed from sitting on the flat-cushioned chair for over an hour. She chose the one closest to the door so that she could rush to the bathroom quickly.

Surrounded by Cecelia's family, she wouldn't dare complain or move; she barely allowed herself to shift. Francesca tried to bring no attention to herself. Mama occasionally came to squeeze her hand or rub circles on her back. But more often than not, she was a flurry of activity, doing whatever she could to make Alma's life easier.

After everything she'd put Cecelia through, it was a surprise Alma and Tony allowed her to wait at all. Their shower of just-starting-something sparklers had been snuffed out in an instant. Francesca felt weak for entertaining the thought, but why her?

Cecelia had kicked and shoved, waited patiently, and held on as she helped crack Francesca's wall. In the end, her perseverance had gotten her a dance, a half-kiss, and a promise of more to come.

Any moment, Alma and Tony would come back, and they'd all leave. Or it could be hours more. The doctor didn't have any straight answers there. Answers about everything else, sure. Whether they should kill Cecelia or not, definitely. But when it came to the length of time it would take for her body to stop working, he had nothing.

A scream echoed down the hall, followed by shouts, alerts, color codes.

Like tense animals, Cecelia's family and close friends rushed towards the noise, Francesca at the head of the pack. When the hoard of nervousness stopped in the hallway in front of her room, the chatter quieted to church whispers. They were only able to peek inside the door. Two nurses had hooked Cecelia to machines she hadn't needed hours ago.

Alma cried out, "Cecelia's alive."

In any other circumstance, loud cheering would have followed. Instead, whispers turned to silence as family and friends took to prayer. The wailing would wait until questions were answered. A bystander-like syndrome took hold of the group as they all stood expecting the others to ask those questions.

"How?" Francesca would not be a bystander.

"They're looking into it. But she screamed, then said, 'Slow'. The doctors were in there by then, so we don't know what's going on. I want to yell at them, make them tell me something, anything! But if they need space to work, they'll have it. Which is why we should go back to the waiting room," Alma responded.

Francesca felt raw. "I can't believe she's alive!"

Mama sidled up beside her and held her hand. She'd become Francesca's strength. Alma would need her the moment they dispersed, but her solidarity meant everything.

"The doctors can't either. Let's wait in the waiting room again. We shouldn't crowd them." Tony became the voice of reason no one wanted.

Francesca stared straight ahead at the ugly strip of yellow

along the walls. Frantic nurses pushing hospital beds of bloodied patients and doctors running into the hallways for those who couldn't wait filled her head. Sloane hadn't made it long enough to be one of those; Cecelia had.

In the waiting room, she sat in the same painful chair and watched Cecelia's family mill about. The clock by the twelve-inch screen television was stuck at 3:12. Francesca wished she could reach that high; she'd take it down, bring it to someone. But who? Nurses wouldn't care, and doctors had better things to do. She'd only seen two receptionists–both perpetually on the phone–barely having a moment to help in-person grieving families.

News of a tornado in Kansas crackled over the Loreti family. Francesca almost laughed. They were certainly not in Kansas. A scarecrow and tin man didn't break out into song, nor did she see any lollipop kids. No good witch showed up to help them make their way to safety either. They were in the eye of the tornado, swirling violently with the cow.

When the doctor came out, the room became a collectively held breath. "She's been sedated. We're going to do some tests and watch her tonight. We don't know what happened, how she... Honestly, it's a goddamned miracle. So let us figure out what we can, and you can come back tomorrow. Smaller groups, please–only two at a time."

Though they all nodded and thanked him, no one stood to leave.

∼

FRANCESCA MADE the second round because she had time before work. At 8:10 am, she stood outside of Cecelia's door. Alma and Tony were already there, waiting.

A different doctor—female with laugh lines around her doe eyes—strode up to them. "Alright, two at a time."

Francesca watched through wavy glass as the Loreti's flanked Cecelia and began talking to her. Unconscious, she didn't answer. Squiggles were happening on the screens of machines they hadn't bothered putting in her room before; that felt positive.

Ten minutes may as well have been ten hours. So, after ten hours, Tony came out and tagged Francesca as if they were in a relay race.

Frail, Cecelia hardly looked like herself. She'd paled to Francesca's coloring, and her sweaty hair had matted against her head.

Alma couldn't let go of her hand, so Francesca felt awkward showing any sign of friendly affection towards Cecelia. Still, she couldn't help but move the hair from her forehead and cheek. "There, that's better." She leaned back and held her other hand.

Cecelia cracked her dark, heavy lashes to reveal her hazelnut eyes, but a shock followed. Her right iris had become an emerald. Francesca didn't shout out, though the inclination was there; Alma didn't seem alarmed. Francesca knew little about comas and even less about essentially coming back from the dead. Who was she to say eyes shouldn't change colors?

A weak smile graced Cecelia's face and her lips crooked to the right. As Cecelia focused on Francesca, her eyes lit up. She'd never looked at her like that before, no one had, except Sloane.

Even in a moment like her friend waking up from a coma, she couldn't shake Sloane from her thoughts. Francesca chastised herself for the umpteenth time. The last year seemed like a roller coaster on a track of disappointments in herself.

Attempting to trace Francesca's palm, Cecelia's hand shook from exertion. "Sloane," she said.

Francesca's chair shook.

"I'm Sloane," she croaked and slipped back into a drug-addled sleep.

Alma stood up quickly. "What did she say? It sounded like she said–" Francesca's heart flew into her throat as she waited for Alma to make sense of it. "–I'm slow. Why would she say that? And in English?" Alma asked, bewildered.

Not exhaling with relief, Francesca replied, "I'm not sure. Maybe you should ask the doctor. I hate to run, especially after that! But I can't be late again. Just because Lia loves me doesn't mean she won't fire me. I'm so glad I was able to see Cecelia, and she could see me before she took another nap. We are all so lucky." It all sounded so insincere and not enough, but there weren't words.

"That we are, dear." Alma squeezed her hand. "If you want to come back tonight, not a lot of people were planning to be here. They're coming during lunch breaks and after school."

"I'd like that." Francesca turned to Cecelia and kissed her on the cheek shakily. "I'll be back tonight. Just rest up. I'll tell you some funny stories when I come."

Numb, she left the hospital to sell pastries and not think about Sloane.

Lia smiled and hugged her when she arrived, even though her shift had started 30 minutes before. "How is she? How are you? How's Alma? And Tony? I'm going before your lunch."

"Uh..." Too many questions, too many words. "She's conscious on and off, but alive. It's a true miracle. And I think the whole lot of us are raw. I'd imagine you feel that way too."

"Too right! I think I'll close up early."

RESTLESS, Lia closed up an hour later with a promise to pay Francesca for the day.

"Take sweets! I made enough for the late morning crowd, so

get what you want. Tomorrow's 'Yesterday's Treats' will be a larger selection than ever! Go, do something for yourself–breathe, meditate, drink, or go back to the hospital. Enjoy today! Miracles don't happen often. Alonzo is picking me up so we can go soon."

"Thank you," Francesca said.

Though she was grateful, a feeling of dread hovered over her. She had to fill time until she could go back to see Cecelia. Hopefully, she wouldn't have to sit in the same burgundy chair. Her back still ached.

⌇

TONY WAVED Francesca in after the nurse told her to go on back. "Look who's awake and alert!" he said with pride as if it had been his accomplishment. "She started talking about being starving about an hour ago. Well, she said the word hungry, but it's a start! She's eaten everything."

Alma corrected, "Except for the fig preserves."

Tony laughed, and agreed, "Yes, except the preserves. I'll be back in a bit. Francesca, could I see you in the hallway for a minute?"

When they were out of earshot, he furrowed his brow. "I thought you'd want a heads-up. They say Cecelia's got selective amnesia. She doesn't remember her childhood; she remembers who I am–Mama too, but not the other family members. She remembers some recent events, too. The doctor said the memories could come back, but it's hard to tell. She's an 'unprecedented case,' he said. So we're just waiting. But either way, she'll be different," Tony explained.

Francesca nodded.

"Her speech should 'normalize' soon too. Right now, she seems to have trouble with some words and her pronunciation is almost as if she doesn't know Italian. Small things seem different too. Did you see her eyes before you left? The right one turned green! The doctors are labeling it heterochromia, though they don't think that fits exactly–nothing does, they say. And if that isn't weird enough, she used to love fig preserves. She would eat anything with a fig, but just now she didn't even open the packet. Considering how inedible the rest of the food was... It was bizarre, but she's alive! Anyhow, if she doesn't recognize you, don't be upset, it may come back. At least she doesn't seem upset by people who are strangers to her, just uncomfortable."

Francesca made a choking sound.

She had planned on saying something, hopefully, something lovely or inspirational, but Tony cleared his throat.

Clearly done talking about it, he said, "Give me a call when you're done visiting. I'm going to go home and change. I didn't remember to do that last night or the night before. I may have worn this for a little while now. I think I'll have a snack, too."

"Maybe a shower and a nap too?" Francesca suggested.

He tugged at his shirt and scrunched his face. "Yes, I think so." He hugged her tightly. "Thank you for being there for her, for our family. We're so glad you're here." Tony kissed her on the cheek.

Her arms were still a little sore from his strength when she sat by an alert Cecelia.

"Francesca," she said as a sigh. Tony was right; she did sound different. At least she remembered her. "I've missed you."

"Missed me? I haven't been gone long. You, on the other hand, have been out for a while."

In English, she said, "You have no idea."

Francesca popped an eyebrow up. "You realize you're speaking English, right?"

Cecelia smiled but pressed on. "It feels like it's been a year." Her mouth crooked to the right again.

"Well, no big changes."

Cecelia held a finger up. "Not exactly true." Her English was incredible.

"You're right. You came back to life," Francesca joked.

"I need to tell you something." The heart monitor beeps sped up.

Francesca wondered if she should get the doctor or if that was an average heart rate. As an adult, shouldn't she know what a healthy heart rate is?

"Of course, anything."

"I'm not Cecelia. I'm Sloane."

Francesca felt as though she'd been slapped. "That's not funny." She was stunned Cecelia would say that, especially in English. Maybe she'd lost her sense of humor. They'd have to work on that together, sooner than later.

"I'm not joking. I'm Sloane. It's me, love."

"Stop it, Cecelia. This is so messed up. I can't imagine what you're going through, but you don't have to take it out on me. And start speaking in Italian again, it's confusing everyone." Francesca stood to leave.

"I'm not lying, Francesca. It's me."

She begged, "Please stop." Still, what she said felt more right than wrong.

"You kept a diary most of your life, but eventually you stopped because you found me. You said you didn't need to tell your secrets to a notebook anymore." Cecelia pulled herself up in the bed a little more. Her hospital gown bunched in the front, and she flattened it down.

Francesca became an antelope.

"You kept those notebooks, though. All of them. Two for each year, one for school and the other for summer. The summer ones are stuffed with movie tickets and wrinkled pool passes. The school ones have photos of your friends and crushes."

Blurred vision cleared as tears trickled down her face. "How do you know that?"

"You know how I know. You said you'd never told anyone about your diaries because then you worried you'd have to lock them. You have all of those locks on a necklace, which is why you didn't want to lock them. You want another? How did I learn Italian? How about the first time we made love? Or how we say we love each other?"

"Stop it."

"No, not after everything I've done to make it back to you. The first time we made love, you wouldn't look into my eyes. You told me it was too scary, that you knew you'd fall so hard you'd never come back up for air if you did. What did I do then, Francesca?"

Her legs gave out, and she thudded into the chair.

"What did I do?"

"Sloane tilted my head up and told me she'd already fallen, so she'd be down there waiting to catch me." Francesca silently sobbed.

"You're my forever, Francesca. I fought to get here. I fought for you. I've missed you; your laugh, your smile, the freckle on the inside of your thigh, your arms around me. I got stuck because I couldn't let go. I could see you, hear you, but I couldn't touch you or talk to you. I've missed our lazy Sundays when you'd somehow convince me that trying a different craft would make me love crafting. I've even missed our arguments. I've gone over every single one. Other than that fucking woman–who still gets to me," she laughed–Cecelia laughed. "They were so stupid! We are perfect for each other, and here you are questioning that it's me! You have to see it; you know it's true. I'm Sloane! I can explain, but first, you have to believe me."

Francesca's head spun. She looked like Cecelia but knew things only Sloane did. It had been Cecelia who'd left her house, who'd gotten in the accident. And yet, those eyes weren't Cecelia's. That smile wasn't Cecelia's.

Francesca had gone crazy. That was it. In one conversation, one short conversation, she'd had a mental break.

33

SLOANE

Physical pain plagued Sloane, and it brought her immeasurable joy. Alive again!

The doctors were more right than they knew when they said Cecelia was a miracle.

Cool, thin sheets rubbed new skin as she shifted in bed. Controlling a new body felt like the time she'd unknowingly eaten a pot brownie before running a 5k. Legs had hit the pavement, arms had swung to keep the momentum, but she'd felt disconnected from her limbs. She'd only had so much control before the universe took over. The universe wasn't helping her now.

Hopefully, time would help connect her to her new body. She would have to thank Molly–if she ever saw her again.

Hopefully, Molly would find someone to live in too, but without taking 'opportunities'. Sloane knew she'd melded first because in some aspects she was stronger than Molly. Though there was also a part of her that knew Molly wanted to be sure it would work.

It would be all for naught if Francesca wouldn't believe her, though. Not running away had been a good start.

"...Other than that fucking woman–who still gets to me. They were so stupid! We are perfect for each other, and here you are questioning that it's me! You have to see it; you know it's true. I'm Sloane! I can explain, but first, you have to believe me," she'd said.

Instantly, she regretted bringing the woman up. They were past it.

Francesca's legs were tense, deciding.

"What else can I say? I can't do much, because Cecelia's body, now my body, is a little broken."

"Did you–" she stopped short. "How di–" Francesca couldn't seem to let herself talk.

A small knock on the door broke both of their concentrations.

"Hi there," a tired nurse in pink scrubs said. "This little one says she has a present for you."

A young bald girl sat in a pink wheelchair. She smiled. "Hi, my name is..." she paused.

"Sarah," the nurse supplied. "Sometimes she gets tired and forgets."

"I have selective amnesia, apparently," Sloane said wryly. "So I get it. It's nice to meet you, Sarah."

She'd have to start speaking in Italian soon; hopefully, Francesca would help her.

She tugged her hospital gown back a little, before she said, "I have a present. I think you will both be pleased with it."

Francesca's snot and salt crusted face didn't change from the frozen shock that made its appearance the first time Sloane had used her real name.

"It's a little muddy," Sarah said with a small chuckle. "But I think you'll find it illuminating."

"What a great word!" the nurse cooed. "Two-dollars worth, at least!"

The little girl turned and stared at the nurse. "Do you think you could leave me for a second?"

"Um, uh, just for a second. I'll be right here at the nurse's station."

Fidgeting with the pens in her shirt pocket, she left.

Sloane smiled at the new Molly expectantly. "You found it?"

"I did. And look!" She spun her chair around with a large smile on her face. "She is in remission now–thanks to me." Molly rubbed her bald head. "So hopefully, I will be here for a long time," Molly said laughing. "Francesca! It is so very wonderful to meet you, finally."

"What?"

"Sloane, you had finished telling her, right? I am not spoiling the reveal?" Molly, the stirrer of pots, asked. "Being alive again is tiring, do you not think?"

Cecelia's head moved almost at the same time Sloane wanted it to when she nodded. "I told her most of it. Just waiting for it to sink in. But thanks for adding more thoughts in the mix," Sloane said sarcastically.

"No problem. It should sink in after this," Molly said confidently and produced the small muddy box. "If you do not believe with this in your hand, then nothing will convince you." She blinked at Francesca.

Sloane grabbed the box from Molly's frail hands. "Thank you."

"Of course. After all, I owe you everything." Her hand reached up to her smooth head again.

"Make sure we don't lose touch. We still have a lot to talk about, you and me. It'll be harder now, but we can do it." Sloane hoped she made Cecelia's face stern.

She already missed her blonde eyebrows.

"What is happening?" Francesca whispered.

"Molly, maybe you should stay. After all, without you, this wouldn't be possible."

The nurse walked in and grabbed the handles of the chair. "Time's up, hon."

"Guess you'll have to tell me about it later." Sarah winked.

Seeing Molly as a different person wasn't strange, but Sloane worried about who she'd picked. Hopefully, she wouldn't hop if Sarah ended up in the hospital again.

"What is that?" Francesca asked, cutting through the image of Molly destroying more lives.

"This is your engagement ring. The night of the accident, I had big plans for us. It's hard to explain how I got it back, but it was always meant to be yours." Sloane pushed back sweaty, foreign black hair and shakily said, "Sorry I can't be on one knee, but... Francesca Lucrezia Nuccio, from the moment I met you, you stole my heart. I knew you'd blow me away, but I couldn't imagine I'd be so lucky as to have you in my life for six years. You are my everything, my one, my only. I don't want to live even one day without you. So I, Susan Allereta Sloane, beg of you, please spend the rest of your life with me. Francesca, my forever, my love, will you marry me?"

Silence.

She'd stunned Francesca speechless. It was too much, too soon. *Of course.*

Sloane had thought things would be the same for Francesca as they were for her, but they were in different places. They'd lived in different worlds for too long.

Francesca sat beside Sloane on the bed. They both shook as Sloane handed the ring to Francesca. What she said next would determine whether all of Sloane's efforts were in vain.

Cheeks going round, Francesca smiled as tears streamed down her freckled face. Resting her forehead on Sloane's, Francesca pressed a kiss to Sloane's new lips.

"I never stopped loving you."

ACKNOWLEDGMENTS

Stories are created by a collection of characters in moments strung together in an order that, hopefully, makes sense. Some people and moments have impacted *my* story in such a profound way that I couldn't thank them enough. A good portion of them are unworthy of being named or mentioned, as being impacted isn't always a positive thing.

There are those who've shaped my story for the better, though. Tessa Garrett has helped me edit every novel I've ever written–even ones I've deleted. I can't count how many hours we've fought over a single comma and the ramifications of keeping it despite it breaking a grammar rule. Thank you for showing me the errors of my ways; I'm better for it.

Sir Scott David Phillips of The Monologue Bombs deserves a huge thank you. Not only did his lyrics appear in this novel, they helped me write it.

Writing dates, as I call them, keep me honest. Without them, I may not have written for weeks. I want to thank my writing partners and friends. They kept me from rewriting every chapter a thousand times, were teachers and sounding boards when I felt lost, and made sure I took breaks–because, sanity.

A beautiful soul named Alexis LT saw me through grief hangover after grief hangover. More importantly, she guided me through realizations of losses. I owe her more than a thank you for her support in my writing and my life.

Jennifer, my sister, is encouraging and loving. Her support has helped me grow in life and writing. I'd laugh less often if she weren't willing to FaceTime at all hours of the day.

Other than giving me life, my parents have always been my cheerleaders. At the ripe old age of 21, Ehlers-Danlos Syndrome caught up to me. As my body betrayed me, they supported me–emotionally and financially–in my decision to switch my focus and energy to writing. I wouldn't be where I am without their love.

My grandmother, who can't read pretty much anything I write because it distresses her, has never faltered in her belief in me. It's unfounded and beautiful.

FINALLY, BUBEE, the incredible, sexy, sarcastic, love of my life. We've lived in a 450 sq. foot apartment and are still happily married; I think that says it all. In case it doesn't, I'll let you in on a not-so-secret fact: I often wonder how I ever smiled before Wes loved me.

Thank you, my love, for being there in every situation–be they perfect or absolutely abysmal. You help me flourish in every sense of the word. I love you.

OH, AND IF I MISSED ANYONE, I'm ever-so-sorry. But know that if we've ever had a conversation–ever, it's possible you should be thanked.

So, thank *you*, strangers, acquaintances, friends, exes. I'd have fewer stories without you.

ABOUT THE AUTHOR

E LIZABETH MITCHELL is an author with Ehlers-Danlos Syndrome drawn to the raw and fantastical. She's happily married to Wes, owned by two Littles, and living in Vancouver, WA. *I Never Stopped* is her debut novel.